WHO RAN MY UNDERWEAR
UP THE FLAGPOLE?

SCHOOL DAZE

Report to the Principal's Office
Who Ran My Underwear Up the Flagpole?

SCHOOL DAZE

WHO RAN MY UNDERWEAR UP THE FLAGPOLE?

JERRY SPINELLI

**Newbery-award-winning author
of *Maniac Magee***

AN
APPLE
PAPERBACK

SCHOLASTIC INC.
New York Toronto London Auckland Sydney

ISBN 0-590-44401-8

12 11 10 9 8 7 6 5 4 3 2 1   2 3 4 5 6 7/9

Printed in the U.S.A.   28

First Scholastic printing, March 1992

For their contributions to this book
I would like to thank Jimmy Kerr, Drumore
Elementary (PA); Charles Patton, principal,
Unionville Middle School (PA); and Karen
Bretzius, whose desserts fueled the writing.

To Betsy Hoffman
  John and Lila McCleary
  Tom and Niki Reeves

WHO RAN MY UNDERWEAR UP THE FLAGPOLE?

1

Eddie Mott remained silent while the debate raged around him.

"He's never coming," said a tall red-haired boy named Wilson.

"He's just late, that's all," said a girl with a skirt on, the only skirted girl in class.

"It's twenty minutes already," said another.

"Maybe he's with the principal."

"Maybe he's sick."

"Maybe he's dead!"

A cheer went up from a dozen students who did not like social studies. Social studies was the subject, Mr. Hollis was the teacher, and he was late. Half the period had passed, and still no Mr. Hollis.

For the first ten minutes no one had said a word. The school year was barely three weeks old, but that had been long enough for the class to learn that Mr. Hollis was not a teacher to mess with. Mr. Hollis believed that kids these days were too pampered and spoiled, and he believed his mission in life was to put a stop to all that.

Physically, Mr. Hollis was perfect for the part: He was the tallest person in the school, his shoulders were wide as two student desks, he had a holler that could rattle glass three classrooms away, and he never, ever smiled. It was a historical fact — though not a surprising one — that Mr. Hollis had never sent anyone to the principal's office, for the simple reason that no one had ever dared to be bad in his class.

If such a student were destined to appear in the future, one thing was certain above all else: That student would not be Eddie Mott. Though he had been a middle school sixth-grader for three weeks now, Eddie was still a grade school kid at heart. He did not feel like a real member of the student body. In the hallways between classes, he felt uncomfortable, edgy, like an outsider among the mobs of clattering seventh-graders and huge, bellowing eighth-graders.

And now he was feeling apart from even his fellow sixth-graders. Where did they get the nerve to talk that way about the dreaded Mr. Hollis? What if he walked in right this second and caught Wilson, the tall redheaded boy, who now was — incredibly — telling the students that they had a right to leave when a teacher was this late?

"I have a brother in college," Wilson was saying, "and if a professor is fifteen minutes late for a class — *zam!*" — Wilson flattened his hand and shot it toward the open door — "they're outta there."

Besides wanting to avoid trouble, Eddie had another reason for not wanting to get "outta there." The reason's name was Sunny Wyler. Ever since he had seen her on the bus heading for the first day of school, Eddie had had this feeling about her. The feeling seemed to be located in his eyes, for whenever she was around, he could not take them off her. And she was around right now. To be precise, she was seated directly across the aisle from him, to his right.

If Eddie could have had his way, he would have swung around, plopped both feet in the aisle, sat sideways in his chair, directly facing her, and stared at her for all forty-five minutes of social studies. Of course, the fearsome Mr. Hollis would never allow such a thing, and neither would Sunny Wyler. Not only did Sunny have no desire to look at Eddie, she did not even like him to look at her.

For the first couple weeks of school, she had been positively mean about it, scowling at him and once even pretending to flick a boogie at him. Then, after he rescued Humphrey, the school's mascot hamster, and returned him to Sunny, Humphrey's caretaker, Sunny had softened a little toward him. But not to the point of allowing him to openly gawk at her.

So Eddie kept his face pointing forward and

jammed his eyeballs to the right till they ached. He wished people came equipped with spare parts. He'd insert his spare eyeball into his right ear and, face forward, look at Sunny Wyler to his heart's content. Since that was impossible, the best he could hope for was to sit beside her for the full forty-five minutes of this period.

But the situation was quickly turning to mutiny.

"How many people have gym next?" demanded Wilson, now standing up front. Almost every hand in the class went up. Eddie, ever obedient, even to a fellow sixth-grader, raised his, too.

"See?" said Wilson. "Who could blame us? Do you think they *want* us to sit here doing nothing, wasting our time? Don't you think they would *want* us to go to the locker rooms now, so we could get a head start changing for gym, so we could be out on the field early, being healthy and all?"

Eddie wasn't surprised at Wilson's line of reasoning. He was known to be a sports fanatic. Even so, his argument seemed to make sense. Nobody was objecting. Eddie sincerely wished somebody would, for he longed to sit beside Sunny Wyler till the last second.

"Look," said Wilson, pointing to the clock, "there's only fifteen minutes left. Do you *really* think he's gonna show up *now*?" He looked over the class; no one answered. He went to the doorway, stuck his head out, looked both ways. He pulled his head back in, swung it toward the class, grinned: "Nobody there."

Several kids giggled.

"I'll even call him, okay?" Wilson stepped fully into the hallway, so he was visible to only the first three rows. But everyone could hear his singsong voice, not as loud as a shout, but louder than a whisper: "Mister Hollll-is . . . Mister *Hollll*-is."

Five seconds of utter silence passed . . . ten seconds. The class, as one, held its breath.

Wilson strode back into the room, beaming, throwing out his arms triumphantly to show that he was safe, he was right. The class applauded.

Wilson seized the moment. He swept his books and gym bag from his desktop, he headed for the doorway, he punched his fist in the air. "Let's go!"

They went. Even Sunny Wyler. Even Eddie Mott, though he was the last one out the door.

Shortly, the boys were pouring into their locker room, the girls into theirs. Eddie found the locker room to be twice as crowded as usual, as the previous class was still there, changing back into school clothes. Eddie plunked his books and gym bag down, sat on the bench, and started getting ready. Like most of the kids, he didn't have to change his sneakers, as he wore his regular school sneaks for gym.

Shouting, laughing, horseplay — the commotion of fifty boys in a sweat-fumed locker room swirled in noisy riot until, in an instant, it stopped, as if snipped by the first syllable of the megaton roar coming from the door: "SOCIAL STUDIES CLASS, THE PERIOD IS NOT OVER! GET BACK WHERE YOU BELONG! THIS IN-STANT! *NOW!*"

The door closed upon dead, stunned silence.

Eddie took off. The man said *NOW!* the man meant *NOW!* He knew it, he *knew* he should never have listened to that Wilson, gone along with the crowd. Well, he may have been the last one out of the room, but he sure wasn't going to be the last one back in. He burst from the locker room, he raced down the hallway even as Mr. Hollis' voice roared into the girls' locker room: *"NOW!"* He careened around corners, flew up a stairway, tore into room 212, social studies, and slammed into his seat so hard he nearly toppled his desk over.

He was gasping, he was shaking, he was ter-rified — but he was also back, the first one back, where he was supposed to be. That should count for something.

Within seconds, Mr. Hollis returned. He glanced once into the room and parked his tow-ering bulk by the doorway, just outside the room. As the other kids began to straggle back, each had to pass beneath his scorching glare. They were quiet and docile as lambs, not a peep, not even from Wilson, who in his haste had neglected to zip up his fly. In spite of the grim situation,

Eddie had to stifle a grin when he saw that.

Apparently others noticed, too, for as they took their seats, Eddie could hear giggles, faint and muffled so as not to reach the ears of Mr. Hollis. Eddie began to feel sorry for Wilson. Somebody should tell him, he thought.

And then Sunny Wyler was coming in, clutching her books, straight-faced — until she sat down and broke into a grin that grew and grew until her mouth was no longer big enough to contain it. Her whole body was shaking, her cheeks were bulging. She managed to do all this in silence, her hand clamped over her mouth, until a most ungirl-like snort, with nowhere else to go, blew out her nose. For his part, Eddie was delighted to see Sunny laughing, since she was usually so grouchy.

All noise and movement came to an abrupt halt as Mr. Hollis stepped into the room and slammed the door shut. He walked slowly to the front-center of the room and folded his arms. When his eyes fell on Eddie, his terrible stare seemed to soften a little. He knows I was the first one back, Eddie thought.

Indeed, as if to confirm this thought, Mr. Hollis spoke: "Never pull that again, people, no matter how late I may be. I want to see every one of you in here after school for a half-hour detention — everyone except" — he looked directly at Eddie — "what's your name, son?"

"Eddie Mott, sir."

"Everyone except Mr. Mott, who obviously was the only one to strictly obey my order to return at once."

Eddie's heart soared.

"Unfortunately," Mr. Hollis went on, "sometimes there's a small price to pay for obedience. Mr. Mott"— he looked not at Eddie but at the clock — "if that clock is correct, you have forty-five seconds before the bell rings and the halls are filled with people . . . forty seconds now to return to the locker room for what you forgot."

Forgot? thought Eddie. Forgot what? He looked from Mr. Hollis to his desk . . . his desk . . . his *empty* desk. No books! He forgot his books!

"Thirty seconds, Mr. Mott."

As Eddie turned sideways to get up, his legs came into view . . . his *legs*. His sneakers were there at the bottom with his socks, and at the top was his red-and-blue Superman underwear, but in between: nothing. *His pants were gone!* Back in the locker room, with his books, abandoned in the terror of Mr. Hollis' *"NOW!"*

"Fifteen seconds, Mr. Mott."

Eddie made it in ten.

2

"**Y**ou're a witness," said Eddie Mott.

"You're loony," said his best buddy, Pickles Johnson.

They were in the alleyway behind Pickles' house after dinner.

"You got the matches?" asked Eddie.

"Yeah."

"The right kind?"

Pickles thrust a box of stick matches in front of Eddie's face. "Yeah, here — okay?"

"Just checking."

Eddie had asked for stick matches because he wasn't sure he could light one of the matchbook types without burning off half his fingers.

"So what do you think?" he said. "Should we pour some gasoline over them, or lighter fluid, or something?"

"Heck no," said Pickles. "Why don't we do it right? Let's steal some TNT and make a bomb and bomb 'em."

9

It took Eddie a second to realize Pickles was joking, and even then he barely cracked a smile. This business was simply too serious to joke about.

At their feet, by the side of the alley, sat a colorful rumpled bundle of underwear — underpants, to be exact. Eddie's entire underpants wardrobe: three Supermans, three Batmans, two Fred Flintstones, and a Casper the Friendly Ghost.

"What are you wearing now?" said Pickles.

Eddie hesitated, then whispered: "Nothing." Just uttering the word made him feel wicked, but grown-up, too, and *that* was the whole idea.

"You *are* loony," said Pickles.

Eddie's ears reddened. His nostrils twitched. It happened whenever he thought about the events of social studies class earlier that day. He poked a finger at Pickles. "Listen, *you* weren't sitting in class in your underwear. *I* was. *You* didn't have to go running through the halls that way. *I* did. It's not *you* everybody in school is laughing about. It's *me*."

"So what are you going to do," said Pickles, grinning, "go streaking down the hallway tomorrow with nothing on just to show everybody you don't wear Superman undies anymore?"

Eddie yanked a wad of dollar bills from a side pocket and thrust it into Pickles' face. "I'm buying new ones with this. I was saving up for comic books."

"So what kind are you going to buy?"

"I don't know."

"Where are you going to get them?"

"I don't know."

"You know anything?"

"Yeah, I know I gotta grow up. I gotta stop being a little kid."

"You *are* a little kid."

"But I *can't* be!" Eddie screeched. "I'm in the middle school now."

"So's everybody else. You're not the only sixth-grader at Plumstead."

Eddie threw up his hands. "Yeah, right, but I *am* the only one who did exactly what the teacher said and went right back to the room, in my underwear. Why didn't anybody *else* do that?"

Pickles grinned. "Because they're not as dumb as you."

Eddie swatted, but Pickles ducked, laughing. "Yeah, well, it's also because I was scared. And why was I scared? Because I act — and think — like a little first-grader. Starting right now — gimme" — he held out his hand; Pickles gave him the matches — "no more baby. No more being laughed at. No more jumping every time a teacher says jump. No more" — he struck a match — "Superman underwear."

He dropped the burning matchstick onto the jumble of underwear. The match burned along the length of itself, swallowed itself, and went out. Eddie struck another match and dropped it; then another and another. The underwear caught, flared. "Yahoo!" went Eddie. Fred Flintstone's face crumpled and dissolved. In less than a minute, the once-bright bundle was a dull, sooty gray, as though the flames had stolen its colors.

Pickles picked up the bucket of water that had been sitting nearby. "Now?"

"No, wait," said Eddie, fascinated to see his little-kidhood going up in smoke.

"That's long enough," said Pickles at last, emptying the bucket. The flames hissed and spat defiantly, then vanished.

"We'll leave it here to make sure it dies out," said Pickles. "I'll scoop it up and put it in a trash can later." He tossed the empty bucket into his backyard. He tugged at Eddie, who was still staring at the smoldering heap. "Come on, snap out of it. We're going to the Acme."

Eddie looked at him. "Acme?"

"Yeah, it's the only place I know around here where you can get yourself some new undies. Let's go, we're riding."

Eddie allowed himself to be steered to the pickleboard, his friend's oversized, custom-made, green, pickle-shaped skateboard. They took off down the alley, Eddie behind Pickles, each with his left foot on the board, right foot pushing, like a pair of oarsmen.

"If you really want to grow up," Pickles called back, "there's something you can try besides new underwear."

"What's that?" said Eddie.

"Go out for football."

3

Salem Brownmiller had a special reason for wanting to make the Plumstead Middle School cheerleading squad. Salem wanted to be a writer. Though strictly speaking, she guessed she was already a writer, if having your very own word processor and your own writing scarf and sitting down and writing practically every day of your life made you a writer — then, yes, she was a writer.

Perhaps you could say she wanted to be a published writer. But then, how about the poem she sent to the children's magazine *Lickity Split*? They had sent her an acceptance letter — she had even kissed the mailman when it arrived — and a month later there it was, on page 19 of *Lickity Split*. Yes, she was already a published writer.

To be really specific about it, what Salem Brownmiller wanted to be more than anything in the world was an *author*. To Salem, the very word itself was magic. *Author*. It meant someone who had written a book, a book that could be found in bookstores and libraries. In Salem's case, the book would be fiction, a story that she would create with her imagination but that would be inspired by real people and real life.

Salem knew that in order to write such books she would have to understand many different kinds of people. She knew that the best way to understand somebody was to put yourself in their place. And that's why Salem Brownmiller was trying out for cheerleading. She knew that the cheerleader was an important kind of person in today's world and that sooner or later she would be writing about one. And since she was not the cheerleading type herself — far from it! — she would have to become one in order to gain insights into the world as seen through the eyes of a cheerleader.

And that's why she had invited her new friend Sunny Wyler over to her house. Sunny was also out for cheerleading.

"I need help bad," said Salem, slumping onto her bed. "I'm the worst one out there. I know I'm not going to make the cut tomorrow." Her eyes rolled hopefully up to Sunny. "Am I?"

Sunny was giving herself a tour of the bedroom, this being her first time in Salem's house. She shrugged. "Probably not."

Salem beat the mattress with her hands and feet. "Ohhhh! You don't have to be so honest."

15

"You asked me."

"You could lie a little."

"You're the greatest cheerleader in the world."

Salem sighed. "What exactly am I the worst at?"

"Everything."

"Ohhh!" Salem clutched her heart as if mortally wounded. Even so, she was glad she had asked Sunny over. Sunny was the only person she could trust to be totally, brutally honest.

"Except maybe for smiling," Sunny added. "You're a pretty good smiler."

"My smile won't keep me from being cut." Salem lay on her back on the bed, staring at the ceiling. She took a deep breath, gathered herself, and sprang to her feet. "Well, let's get started. I brought you here because you're the best of all the sixth-graders. To tell you the truth, I think you're better than the seventh- and eighth-graders, too."

Sunny seemed oblivious to the compliment. She pulled from Salem's bedstead a length of black, silky material. "What's this?"

"My writing scarf," said Salem. "I always wear it when I'm writing." To demonstrate, she took the scarf from Sunny, flung it once around her neck, sat down at her keyboard, and pretended to peck away. "Tah-dah. I write my stories and poems here, then transfer them to my father's desktop publisher."

"You're goofy," said Sunny.

"Thank you," Salem replied primly. "I hope so. Actually, the word you're looking for is *eccentric*, which is what writers are supposed to be."

"And what's all the posters?" said Sunny, gazing at one.

"Paris. That's the Eiffel Tower. That one over there is the famous Left Bank."

"Famous for what?"

"Famous for writers. That's where all the American writers went back in the 1920s. A couple of years on the Left Bank, and they became famous. I'm just getting started in here. Pretty soon, when you walk in here you'll think you're right in the middle of the Left Bank of Par-*ee*."

"You're not goofy," said Sunny, "you're weird."

Salem got up. She tossed her writing scarf aside. "I am also going to be cut from cheerleading tomorrow if you don't help me out."

Sunny just stared at her. "Am I *that* hopeless?" Salem asked. Sunny kept staring.

Even considering Sunny's unusual first name — the official version of which was Sunshine — Salem sometimes wondered why she liked Sunny. Sunny's disposition was often anything but. She always seemed to be complaining or otherwise looking on the dark side of things. She was, to put it bluntly, a grouch.

And yet there was something appealing about her. Most of the time she made you want to laugh instead of being grouchy back. Two of Salem's other friends, Eddie Mott and Pickles Johnson, liked Sunny, too. In fact, Eddie *really* liked her, though Sunny was as cool to him as she was to all boys. I wonder if she likes me, Salem thought.

At last Sunny said something: "Coochy Coo."

Salem groaned. "Oh, no. That's my worst one."

"That's why you should work on it." Sunny snapped her fingers. "Let's go."

All of the routine was regular cheerleading moves except for the "Coochy Coo" lines of the chant. As Ms. Baylor, the cheerleading coach, had demonstrated, you had to do a wiggle while at the same time make a full-circle turn.

Salem stood in the middle of her room, unmoving.

"Let's go," Sunny repeated. "Coochy . . ."

Salem took a deep breath and plunged in:

"Coochy Coochy Coochy COO!
We're gonna win.
Well, it's TRUE!
Coochy Coochy Coochy COO!
We're gonna win.
We're gonna beat YOU!"

It ended with an aggressive stomp forward with one foot and a thrust of the forefinger at the other team, wherever they were. Sunny blinked for a while, looked at her feet, then at the wall posters.

"Well?" said Salem.

Sunny sniffed. "Your finger point wasn't bad."

"And the rest?"

Sunny held her nose.

"I *know* it stinks!" Salem cried out. "That's why you're here, to help me unstink myself. You have" — she looked at her digital clock — "an hour and fifteen minutes to make me a better cheerleader. Show me. Coach me."

Sunny stared steadily at her. "If I had to pick the worst of the worst, it would be the wiggle."

"Really bad, huh?"

"The pits. I've seen better wiggles on boys."

"Acchhh!" Salem flung herself back to the bed. "What's the matter with me? When I make myself into a character in a story, I'm always so graceful and elegant. Why can't I be like that in real life? What kind of a girl am I? Eleven years old, and I can't even wiggle yet!" She pounded her pillow and buried her face in it.

A silence followed. Then Salem felt the mattress sag: Sunny had sat on the bed. Then came Sunny's voice, in a flat, I'm-not-impressed tone: "Aren't you overdoing it a little?"

Salem couldn't help it, she laughed into her pillow. She swung onto her back. "That's what my parents always say, I overdo it. I guess if I weren't a writer I'd be an actress." She sat up. She was liking Sunny more and more, grouch or not. "But I really *do* have to make cheerleading.

So I can find out what makes a cheerleader tick. So I can get *insights*."

Salem looked down. She hadn't realized it, but she was clutching Sunny's arm, as if to squeeze the cooperation out of her. Sunny was looking back, still unsmiling, but with no sign of discomfort or disapproval. Salem knew that Sunny was not the type of girl that just anybody could touch, much less grab; yet Sunny sat calmly, patiently, and made no move to extract her squeezed arm. In that moment Salem began to understand the language upon which their friendship would be traded. Yes, she thought, she does like me.

4

Sunny tried. Salem tried. But it was not to be. The following day, standing in the grass by the sideline, the pads of the practicing football teams thumping in the background, Salem listened in vain as Ms. Baylor called out the names of the survivors. Sunny, of course, made it, despite Ms. Baylor's constant harping: "Smile, Wyler, smile!"

Sunny stayed close to Salem as the girls headed for the gym to pick up their books. The lowering sun, whose age was reckoned in the millions of years, sat upon the roof of Plumstead Middle School, not yet one month old.

"Now what?" Sunny asked.

Salem only shrugged.

The route to the gym took the girls along the perimeter of the football field, which was occupied by two teams: the varsity and the 100-pound. The latter was made up entirely of sixth- and seventh-graders.

The girls skirted the goalposts at one end and were coming up the opposite sideline when several players began dashing their way. The football had been fumbled and was wobblehopping over the grass, the players in frantic pursuit, as though chasing a rabbit. They all caught up with it at once, and the resulting collision of helmets and bodies caused several of the girls to stop and gasp.

The knot of players, each grasping for the ball, lurched and staggered like a drunken, many-headed creature. Suddenly the whole knot spun violently, and out of it came one of the players flying and landing with an "Oof!" at the feet of Salem and Sunny.

The player's number, 89, was so big for his body that the bottoms of the 8 and the 9 were buried in his padded pants. His glossy purple helmet also seemed enormous for the thin, pale stalk of a neck showing beneath it.

Number 89 groaned, a bleating, high-pitched sound that did not seem to go with the huge pads that bloated the shoulders of his shirt. He pushed himself to his knees, to his feet, and suddenly he was screaming, "I can't see! I can't see!"

At that point he was standing directly in front of Sunny, his voice coming through the purple plastic helmet, rather like that of a giant talking fly. "No kidding, you dummy," said Sunny, plucking the helmet from the head. "Your helmet got turned backwards."

"Eddie Mott!" exclaimed Salem.

Eddie Mott's eyes gaped as if he were newly hatched. "Sunny," he breathed.

Sunny dropped the helmet into his hands. "Here's your head back."

"You're bleeding," Salem said, rushing in. A gash across the bridge of Eddie's nose was spilling blood. "He's bleeding!" she called to the field. In an attempt to stop the flow, she pressed the short sleeve of her shirt to his nose. To someone at a distance, it would have looked like a girl giving a boy a whiff of her underarm.

In time Mr. Lujak, the coach, came clomping over, not exactly in a big hurry. "What now?" he growled.

Salem took her arm away. "He's bleeding. It's cut."

Eddie himself seemed not to notice the injury but kept gazing at Sunny.

"Great," said the coach. "I got a halfback over there who thinks he's got a loose tooth. I got a center who giggles every time the quarterback touches his rear end. And I'm supposed to get this team ready to play somebody two weeks from now." He looked up and down the sidelines. He shouted in the direction of the school, the ancient sun: "I need a manager!"

In a flash of recovery and inspiration, Salem Brownmiller shot her hand skyward. "I'm here!"

5

T. Charles Brimlow, brand-new principal of brand-new Plumstead Middle School, welcomed his guests into his office: Salem Brownmiller, Sunny Wyler, Eddie Mott, and Dennis "Pickles" Johnson. The Principal's Posse, he called them. He had invited these four sixth-graders to have lunch with him on the first day of school and had decided to make it a weekly occasion.

The first two lunches had been fancy, cafeteria-catered affairs. Now, over Salem's objections, it was just bring your brown bag and sit wherever you like.

Mr. Brimlow himself stood, leaning back against the front edge of his desk. Eddie Mott fished into his bag from his seat on the rug. "What happened there, Eddie?" said the principal.

Eddie touched the adhesive bandage that humped over the bridge of his nose and tailed under both eyes. "Football." He said the word with a clear hint of pride, then added with a casual shrug, "No problem."

The principal assumed that this manly performance was for the benefit of Sunny Wyler, whom Eddie liked. As for Sunny, chomping a sandwich in one of the high-backed leather chairs, she was plainly unimpressed. So Brimlow, not wanting Eddie to go scoreless, raised his own eyebrows. "Football, huh? Tough sport."

"Nah," said Eddie, ripping a chunk from his Devil Dog as though he were an animal eating raw meat. "You gotta play with a little pain, that's all."

"He was bleeding all over at practice yesterday," said Salem, who had settled into the other leather chair. "He was *gushing*. I had to stop it with my shirt, which I had to throw away because it was half-dyed red. Ugh!"

"And what were you doing on the football field?" asked Mr. Brimlow.

"That's a long story," Salem said, and everyone knew that no one could stop Salem from telling it. "I was trying out for cheerleading so I could gain new insights so I could be a better writer, someday an author of books, as you know. I feel that as a writer, it's important to get into your main character as much as possible."

"She bombed out," said Sunny, munching.

Salem stared wide-eyed across the office at her

friend, blinked, turned back to the principal. "I didn't make the cut. I — "

"She can't wiggle."

"Sunny!" White bread specks flew from Salem's mouth. She fumed, glared, squeezed her sandwich, giving it a twist. At length she regained her composure and turned again to the principal. "I guess I'm not the most coordinated person in the world, at least not in a cheerleading kind of way. Anyway, I didn't make it, and practice was over, and we were walking around the field when — *pow* — there's this big collision of players, and one of them lands at our feet — of me and my *former* friend, Miss *Sun*shine Wyler" — she said, knowing Sunny hated that name — "and who was it but Eddie Mott."

"Bleeding," said Mr. Brimlow, hoping to hasten the story.

"Gushing," Salem nodded, "but we didn't know it at the time because he had his helmet on backwards, which my former friend pulled off. Then the blood. And the sleeve. And then Mr. Lujak, the coach, came over and complained that he needed a manager to help him out and I said, 'Hey, that's me!' "

"Now you're gaining insights into football managers," offered Mr. Brimlow.

"Exactly," said Salem, still holding a full sandwich minus one bite. "They may not be as important in the world as cheerleaders, but that doesn't mean they're not interesting."

"Especially," snickered Sunny, "if the manager gets a load of Eddie's underwear."

Eddie nearly choked on the last bite of his second Devil Dog. "Hey, what's that supposed to mean?"

Sunny's eyes wandered over the ceiling. "It's a bird . . . it's a plane . . . it's — "

Eddie spluttered, "That was a mistake! I don't have Superman underwear!"

Sunny gave Eddie's beltline a sly, sideways leer. "Oh, no?"

"No!" squawked Eddie, rising to his knees and facing Sunny. His ears were red, his nostrils twitching.

Mr. Brimlow froze. Was the boy going to prove it?

"It's true," said Pickles, speaking for the first time. He sat in the principal's swiveling armchair, which he had wheeled out alongside the desk. His pickle-green sneakers were propped up at the heels and crossed casually on the carpet. "The underwear was an old pair left over from when Eddie was little. He only wore them that day because all the others were in the wash."

Eyes paddleballed between Pickles and Eddie. Brains computed this new claim.

No one really believed it, a conclusion voiced

by Sunny's sarcastic snort: "Yeah, right."

As far as Mr. Brimlow was concerned, believing it was beside the point. What touched him was Pickles' attempt to rescue his pal from ridicule.

Eddie, his face grimly set, was on his feet now. He went behind the high-backed chair in which Salem sat. Visible only from the neck up, he appeared to be twisting, doing something. A brief ripping sound was heard. Eddie emerged from behind the chair. He marched straight to Sunny and threw a small, white something into her lap. "Here."

Sunny looked at it. She burst out laughing. She flung the white thing back at Eddie. It sailed, as if on the wind of her laughter, past Eddie and came to rest at Mr. Brimlow's feet. He picked it up. It was the cloth label from Eddie's underwear. It read *FRUIT OF THE LOOM*.

"Well," Mr. Brimlow said, searching for words to put a lid on this episode. "This certainly has been a revealing lunchtime."

Sunny said, almost in a whisper, "He thinks he's all grown up."

Mr. Brimlow stared at her, his expression saying, Give it up, Sunny, back off; but she was speaking into her lap: "How big can he be if he eats his Devil Dogs first?"

She ended with a brief snicker. No one joined in. She snickered some more, alone. "Well, *I* think it's funny."

Eddie Mott sat alone on the carpet, staring blankly at an empty Devil Dog wrapper.

For once Salem was at a loss for words. Mr. Brimlow himself searched his mind for a way to repair the damage he has just witnessed. His impulse was to rush over to Eddie Mott and take the kid in his arms and tell him it was okay. Since the first day of school, when a group of eighth-graders had tossed him around the school bus, Eddie had been picked on — and now by no less than a fellow sixth-grader. And the boy was the timid type to begin with. Mr. Brimlow had the crazy feeling that if he did not say or do something useful in the next two seconds, Eddie Mott would dissolve, right before their eyes, into a puddle on the rug.

And then the matter was taken out of his hands. Pickles Johnson pulled a Devil Dog from his lunch bag. "Eddie," he called and tossed it.

Eddie stabbed at the pack one-handed, missed, picked it up. He looked over at Pickles, and something in his face changed. He unwrapped the Devil Dog. He stared at the chocolate sandwich. He pulled the halves apart, revealing the pure white creamy filling. He glanced once again at Pickles, stood, walked over to Sunny in her high-backed chair, and mashed one of the chocolate cake halves, creamy side down, into her face.

The bell rang as Pickles, Salem, and Eddie erupted into gales of laughter. They gathered up their lunch trash and dropped it into the waste-basket; then they hung around, still chuckling, while Sunny scooped filling from her face and licked away every fingerful. She nodded. "Mm . . . thanks." She pulled a napkin from her bag, wiped her face dry, got up, tossed her trash into the basket, and went out with the others.

For more than a minute the principal just stood there, trying to figure out what he had just seen. Where did Eddie get the nerve to do it? Why didn't Sunny retaliate? Why didn't she even seem to be upset? With his foot Mr. Brimlow pushed his swivel chair back behind his desk. Apparently he still had a lot to learn about sixth-graders.

6

"**N**o! No! No! . . . This way! . . . *This* way!"
All afternoon the voice of Arnold Hummelsdorf could be heard braying over the playing fields of Plumstead, louder than the football coaches, louder than the cheerleaders. Hummelsdorf, known to generations of Cedar Grove students as Lips, was the school's music director.

Only two weeks before, Hummelsdorf had achieved the unbelievable: For the musical segment of the opening assembly, he had directed onstage a band that was composed of every student of the new school — all 340 of them, playing the likes of soda bottles, washboards, and rubber bands. The auditorium seats had been empty of everyone but teachers.

In the afterglow of that stunning achievement, Hummelsdorf had hatched another. Plumstead would be the first middle school in the county — or anywhere, so far as he knew — to put a marching band on the field during halftime of football games, especially 100-pound-team games. Well, he got his band, all right — all seven of them. A bugle player, a tuba player, a clarinetist, a triangle player, a flutist, a drummer, and a violinist. The violinist, of course, belonged in the school orchestra, but the kid volunteered to march, and Hummelsdorf was only too happy to get every warm body he could. He would have taken a flute-tooting duck had one presented itself.

Once, Lips Hummelsdorf had dreamed of leading 200-member bands before vast crowds in college stadiums. Instead he had come to this, trying to teach seven nincompoops how to march and play at the same time. Well, six actually; the bugler, the kid called Pickles, wasn't so bad.

The others were a horror story. The flutist was forever turning the wrong way and bumping into the clarinetist. At one point, the violinist dropped her bow. When she stopped and stooped to pick it up, the tubist, marching onward, went flying over her back and landed head-down into the gaping mouth of his own instrument. For a half second there, before the kid toppled over, it looked as though a student were being swallowed headfirst by a great white tuba.

The triangle player, a sixth-grader as tiny as the *ting* from his instrument, seemed in a total fog, as though he were supposed to be elsewhere, maybe Mars. In any case he kept marching off in odd directions — *ting ting ting* — and Hummelsdorf had to keep calling him back: ". . . *this* way!"

But worst by far was the drummer. To begin with, he was an eighth-grader, meaning he thought he owned the school and all surrounding property.

As if that wasn't bad enough, he was also one of these so-called nickelheads. The trouble kids went to these days to make themselves ugly, especially with their hair, was beyond Hummelsdorf. Glopping it, slicing it, spiking it, roasting it — he had seen hair in the hallways that would terrify a werewolf. And now these nickelheads, with their teddy bear cuts and circles gouged out right down to the skull. To Hummelsdorf, it looked as though an octopus had grabbed each of them by the head.

And now, recently, some of them had taken to painting the bald circular patches. If they wanted to be clowns, why didn't they go join the circus? And this one, the drummer, was probably the most ridiculous of all. His head circles were not only painted, they were numbered. All he needed was a cue stick and he could play pool with his own head. And in fact his nickname was Cueball.

The nickelhead imagined himself to be a drummer with a famous rock band and was totally out of control. He beat not only his own snare drum but anything else that came within reach: the triangle player's triangle, the tuba, the violinist's head, his own head. In the nickelhead's hands, the drumsticks became instruments of mayhem. He tickled Pickles' stomach as he was tooting, changing bugle notes to a horse's whinny. He stuck the tip of a drumstick into the clarinetist's ear and up the flutist's nose.

And now he was over by the cheerleaders, bothering them. The remaining six members of the band could not contain their curiosity. In the middle of the fight song, composed by Hummelsdorf himself and called "Hail to the Hamsters," the band stopped their marching and turned toward the cheerleaders. The notes from their instruments subsided to a trickle. "Play! Play!" ranted Hummelsdorf, but when he himself turned to see what was happening, the music ceased altogether.

What they saw were the cheerleaders doing their wiggle-waggle Coochy Coo number, and behind them the nickelhead thumping away on his drum and doing a wild, comical wiggle of his own. Then he sneaked up behind one girl in particular and started tapping with his drumstick where she wiggled. The girl whirled — it was Sunny Wyler — whacked him in the chops with a roundhouse right, and began chasing him over the grass.

"Don't come back, nickelhead — knucklehead — whatever your name is!" yelled Hummelsdorf. "You're off the band!" The only reply from Cueball was a shrieking cackle as he unhitched his drum from his belt and fled onto the football field barely ahead of the raging cheer-leader.

Meanwhile Eddie Mott was doing some running of his own. He was playing second-string halfback against the first-string 100-pounders. He had taken the ball on a handoff from the quarterback and suddenly — miraculously — found himself in the clear, nothing between him and the goal line but thirty yards of green grass.

Just as he was beginning to believe in his good luck, it turned bad. Racing for the goal, his eye caught a movement beyond the edge of his bob-bing, too-big helmet. He gripped the ball tighter and turned, bracing to be tackled. But instead of a first-string 100-pounder in a football uniform, he saw to his amazement a nickelhead shrieking and waving a pair of sticks.

Since the first day of school, the nickelheads had been a pestilence upon Eddie. Time and again they made him pay a lunch tax, usually the dessert from his lunch bag. They took every other op-portunity to harass him. He had thought that on the football field at least he would be safe; but now, here was this nickelhead galloping straight toward him, and all Eddie could think was, Oh, no!

He forgot about the goal line, he forgot about the football — he flung it away and just took off in the opposite direction. If Eddie had looked back, he would have seen Cueball continue running across the field and toward the school. But he did not turn, he simply ran, sure that any moment now the nickelhead's hand would reach out and grab him by the neck. He did not realize that he was running onto the varsity team's portion of the practice field. Neither did he realize that a critical part of his uniform was coming loose.

By the time Eddie had belatedly come out for football, all the 100-pound uniforms had been taken. All that remained was one varsity uniform, intended for a 200-pound tackle, number 89. The tail of the shirt came down to his knees, the helmet felt as roomy as a watermelon, and the pants he could have wrapped twice around his waist. The pants did not use a belt but cinched with a drawstring — and Eddie had never been good at tying knots.

Now, unbeknownst to him as he fled the phantom nickelhead, the drawstring knot was coming loose. With every frantic step, it got a little looser. Eddie never noticed, partly because he was overcome with panic, and partly because his oversized football uniform had always felt loose as a tent. Consequently, Eddie was as surprised as everyone else when suddenly his pants collapsed about his ankles and sent him sprawling onto the grass.

The nearest varsity players to him at that moment were the defensive linemen, who were working out on the dummy sled. As Eddie spit out grass and turned, expecting to see a crazy nickel-head about to pounce on him, he saw instead the hugely grinning face of Richard "Tuna" Casseroli, the biggest player on the team, the biggest kid in the school, second in size only to the titanic social studies teacher, Mr. Hollis.

The next thing Eddie knew, he was being hoisted by his ankles, the early October air cool on his bare, white legs. To his eyes, inches from the ground, the world was a vast carpet of green grass, while far above, the voice of Tuna Casseroli boomed: "Hey, look — no Supermans! No Supermans!"

7

The late bus grumbled softly in the parking lot, awaiting the last of the football and field hockey players and cheerleaders and band members to climb aboard. Eddie had no intention of taking the late bus. After this latest disgrace, the last thing he needed was to board a bus and find himself staring into fifty grinning, sniggling faces.

He dawdled in the locker room, finding all sorts of little things to do before changing his clothes. By now he was positively paranoid about being undressed. His bare body was better known to his schoolmates than that of anyone except Humphrey the hamster, Plumstead's mascot. He imagined that eyes — eighth-grade eyes, nickelhead eyes — were constantly watching him, and that the instant he took off his clothes they would swoop down and scoop him up and fling him out into the middle of the football field for all the world to see.

And so he dawdled while the others horseplayed

and showered and changed. Finally the last one left. He was alone. Wasn't he? He checked the aisles of lockers, the showers. Yes, alone.

Even so, he decided to take as few chances as possible. Normally, for the last eleven years, or ever since he took over for his mother, his pattern was this: get totally undressed, then dress. No more. Never again. From this day forward, Edward Mott would never as long as he lived leave more than one body part exposed at any one time.

Thus he took off the right football shoe and sock, put on the right sock and sneaker; took off the left football shoe and sock, put on the left sock and sneaker; and so on. And even this he did as quickly as possible, glancing around all the while. Once he even stood on the bench to check out the tops of the lockers in case anyone was lying flat up there, waiting.

The parking lot was right outside the locker room. Several high, frosted windows were open, and through them Eddie could hear two voices in a most unusual shouting match:

"I said you're out!"

"Aww, come on, let me back in!"

"No!"

"I'll be good!"

"No!"

"Aww, Lips, please!"

"Never!"

The voices obviously belonged to a student and

to Mr. Hummelsdorf, the band director. Everybody called Mr. Hummelsdorf "Lips" behind his back, because of his plumlike lower lip, turned out and dangling from forty years of showing students how to play the trumpet, the trombone, and his favorite, the tuba. So far as Eddie knew, this was the first time anyone had ever said "Lips" to his face, and at the sound of it Eddie could feel the universe tense up. Certainly he himself did, pausing for the only time during his quick change.

When he finally left the locker room, he went to the side door and peeped out, just in time to see the late bus pulling out. Carefully, he opened the door and stepped onto the parking lot macadam. For half a minute he stayed there, near the door, like a mouse by his hole, alert, sniffing for any sign of the cats of his existence, eighth-graders and nickelheads.

All he saw was the flat, gray tableland of the parking lot; all he heard was the faint rush of traffic from the distant street. He clutched the drawstring sack containing his books and football shirt, took a deep breath, and ventured out. A clatter arose to his right, making him freeze; then a yelp; then from around the brick corner of the building came a sight out of a Saturday morning cartoon.

It was the same shape and color as the pickleboard — only much larger. It was the biggest, the longest skateboard he had ever seen. It had six wheels. It carried three people — Sunny, Salem, and Pickles — all of them laughing and yelping as Pickles guided the enormous green vehicle up to him.

All Eddie could say was, "Wow."

"Wow squared!" laughed Salem.

"What *is* it?" said Eddie.

With the tip of his sneaker, Pickles pointed to the yellow lettering on the curved, green side panel. It read:

PICKLEBUS

"Once was a surfboard," said Pickles. "Now it's our own private late bus. The four of us. I've been working on it for weeks. I just finished it last night." Pickles went on to explain that a friendly custodian had allowed him to park the picklebus in the basement. He slapped the side panel. "Climb aboard."

The two girls backed up, leaving a space between Pickles and Salem. Eddie climbed on. He could see now that only one side of the board had a side panel; the right side had been left open for shoe-to-sidewalk locomotion.

"Here we go!" called Pickles, pushing off from his pilot's position.

"Tallyho!" called Salem.

And off they went, three times in a wide circle around the parking lot — four legs pushing off like oars in unison, a pickle-shaped galley on an asphalt sea — then once around the school and down the driveway to the sidewalk.

They cruised along slowly to the *clack-clack* of the sidewalk cracks, making the ride last. They were, from front to back: Pickles, Eddie, Salem, Sunny.

Salem tapped Eddie on the back, "Did you hear the argument?"

"Yeah," said Eddie. "It sounded like Mr. Hummelsdorf and some kid."

"That knucklehead jerk, Cueball," came Sunny's snort from the rear.

"Did I hear right?" said Eddie. "He called Mr. Hummelsdorf — " Eddie hesitated to say it.

"Lips?" Pickles nodded. "Yep. Cueball was on the bus, leaning out the window. Mr. Hummelsdorf was getting into his car. That's when they got into it. Cueball said it, right to his face, halfway out the bus window. Lips."

Eddie got the shivers just picturing it. "Wow."

"That's a nickelhead for you," said Pickles.

"That's one *dead* nickelhead for you," said Sunny.

"Ski jump!" shouted Pickles, and all four screamed as the picklebus flew off a high curb and landed five feet into the street, everyone teetering for balance but still aboard. "Yeah!" they cheered, pumping their fists in the air.

8

There was no ramp up to the next sidewalk, so the riders had to halt the picklebus and lift it over the curb. When they got back on, the order from front to back had changed. Now it was: Pickles, Salem, Eddie, Sunny.

The new order was no accident. At least, not on Salem's part.

When they reboarded the bus, Salem quickly inserted herself right behind pilot Pickles, leaving the third slot, in front of Sunny, open. Salem did this for a very clear reason: She knew that Eddie liked Sunny, so she figured she would arrange for him to be close to her.

As for Eddie, he knew that Salem knew that he liked Sunny; so when he saw that his place had changed, he didn't argue, he took it. As the Posse pushed off, Eddie put his hands on Salem's waist to hold steady, as Salem was doing to Pickles. He tingled, waiting for the touch of Sunny's hands on his own waist. A block went by. The touch never came.

Oh, well, Eddie wasn't surprised. Sunny was a notorious boy-hater, so what could he expect? He was glad she wasn't poking him in the ribs or jumping off and walking home. He was glad just to know she was right behind him, *that* close.

There may or may not have been another reason why Salem changed places when reboarding the bus — it was not clear, least of all to Salem herself. She thought all she was doing was a favor to Eddie. But then, when she found herself close behind Pickles as they hummed down the sidewalk, and when she put her hands on his waist, even she wasn't sure if she was doing it just to hang on.

"So," she said, blowing away her dimly disturbing feelings, "what did everybody think of the big announcement today?"

"About the cookie sale?" said Eddie.

"No," scoffed Salem, "the Halloween dance."

Principal Brimlow had announced that on the last Friday in October — otherwise known as Halloween — there would be a school dance. What the principal did not say was that the dance was intended to keep the older kids off the streets that night. Too many neighbors were complaining about rowdy teenagers merely holding masks in front of their faces and demanding unreasonable amounts of candy. What the principal did say was that everyone who came in a costume would get a bag of treats.

"I'm not going," said Sunny. "Why would I want to go to a dance?"

"To dance with boys," Pickles called back, kidding.

"I'd rather dance with crocodiles."

"Eddie, how about you?" said Salem.

Eddie hesitated before finally answering, "I don't know. I'll have to think about it." Which was the truth. After hearing the announcement that day, Eddie had prompty forgotten it. It didn't seem to apply to him. He could not imagine himself going to something as grown-up as a dance. Sometimes it was hard to believe that he wasn't still back in grade school. Yes, this was going to take a lot of thinking.

"Well, isn't *anyone* going?" Salem whined. She tweaked the pilot in the waist. "How about you?"

"I don't know, either," said Pickles. "I hate to give up trick-or-treating. I'll think about it along with Eddie." He raised his right arm, then extended it to the side. "Right full rudder!" The picklebus veered to the right, rolled down a grassy slope, and coasted onto the asphalt playground of his old school, Second Avenue Elementary.

But Salem wasn't finished. Frustrated at her friends' unsatisfying answers about the dance, and discovering that something in her fingers liked the feeling of tweaking Pickles' waist, she began to tickle him.

"Hey," Pickles protested as the bus shimmied. "Stop!"

"Not until somebody agrees to go to the dance with me," said Salem, tickling harder.

"No . . . no!" Pickles laughed, trying to protect himself and control the bus, which now swung wildly, as though *it* were being tickled, four right paddle feet stabbing at the ground — "we're gonna — "

The crash came before the word; the bus yawed sharply, sailed atilt for two breathless seconds on the three left wheels, and plunged into a railroad tie at the edge of the grass surrounding the asphalt.

Three of them got up, unhurt.

"Sunny!" cried Salem.

Sunny had landed in a play area truck tire. Only her legs were sticking out. The other three raced over and peered into the round, rubbery well of the enormous tire.

"Sunny?" whispered Salem.

Sunny opened one sleepy eye. She groaned. "I'm dead."

Salem and Pickles laughed with relief. Eddie Mott did not. "What's so funny?" he scolded. "She's injured." Pangs of worry and a crush of love brought panic to his eyes. "We gotta get her to a doctor!"

He reached into the tire well, gripped Sunny under the arms, and pulled her to a sitting position on the tire's broad sidewall.

"Let her sit there. She's woozy, that's all," said Pickles, laid-back as ever.

"That's *all*?" screeched Eddie. "She could go into a coma any second. Look at her!" They looked at her. She did not look back. Eddie raised one of her eyelids. The three of them leaned in. "What do you think?" said Eddie.

Pickles shrugged. "It's an eyeball."

They stared at the gaping, blinkless eyeball for a while, but no one could think of anything more to say about it. Eddie let the lid drop. He had to hold her up, for her entire body was limp, without bones, it seemed. A groan came from deep inside her.

"That's it," said Eddie firmly. "I'm getting her to a doctor, with or without you people. Her brain could be losing oxygen right now. She could be a vegetable in minutes." He reached into the tire well, pulled out her legs, and swung them around till they hung outside the tire. He then crouched, leaned his shoulder into her midsection, wrapped his arms around her, and straightened up. He could hardly believe it — it worked! He was carrying her. She was draped over his shoulder, like a sack, just like in the movies.

Unfortunately, this was true only as long as he stayed still. As soon as he tried to move, he discovered that, due to the body on his shoulder, he was seriously lopsided to the right. He began to tilt in that direction. He threw out his right leg to brace himself, stopping the sideways tilt, only to find himself now tilting backwards. He planted his left foot and attempted to heave himself forward. He succeeded, but only with himself, for as his shoulders came forward, the slumped body continued its slide backwards, smoothly, unstoppably flowing over his right shoulder and down his back and onto the grass.

At this point Pickles made a move to intervene but was stopped by Salem, who was overcome by the exquisite romance of it all: Eddie Mott gallantly struggling to save the girl who rejected him. Practically in tears, she held Pickles by the arm. "Let them go. Let him try."

Eddie tried. Sunny was a groaning human puddle at his feet. This time he decided he would carry her the old-fashioned way, like men carry their brides over the threshold. He bent, he stooped, he squatted. He wormed his arms under her, one arm under her legs at the knees, the other under her back. He tried to remember how those Olympic weight lifters did it. He spread his feet, squared his shoulders, straightened his back. He braced himself, he took a deep breath, he lifted, he farted. Sunny never left the ground.

"That does it," said Pickles, pulling away from

Salem. He righted the overturned picklebus. "Help me out."

Together, Pickles and Salem lifted Sunny into the picklebus and started pushing her up the hill to the street. Eddie gathered everyone's books and followed.

Maybe it was the ride, maybe it was escaping Eddie's care — whatever, within a block Sunny was sitting up. Within two blocks she was her old self, grouching, "Did I *imagine* some dumbo dumped me on my head?"

9

When Salem Brownmiller became student manager of the Plumstead 100-pound football team, Mr. Lujak, the coach, outlined her primary duties as follows: "Wash the uniforms after game days, be ready with the first-aid kit, and just generally help out." That last part gave Salem all the leeway she needed. With it, she took student management to places where no one had ever taken it before.

It began the day after Eddie Mott lost his pants. Salem, who had witnessed the whole episode, knew what the problem was. As Eddie trotted onto the practice field next day, Salem called him over. She sat on the bench, made him stand in front of her, and started to untie the drawstring that cinched the waist of his oversized pants.

"Hey — " he protested, slapping her hands. "What are you doing?"

She pushed his hands away. "I'm tying you a good knot."

Eddie glanced about nervously. "You can't." The last thing he needed was to have other guys see him being dressed by someone else, a girl no less. He pushed her hands away.

Salem grabbed his arms by the wrists and clamped them to his sides. "*Listen* — do you want me to tie you a knot that won't come undone, or do you want your pants to fall down again today?"

Eddie squeaked and fidgeted in frustration, but he let her tie the knot. The moment she finished, he took off — and then it happened. Quite unexpectedly, before she could rise from the bench, Salem found herself facing another football player. It was Raymond Milford, a sixth-grader and one of the littlest kids on the team.

"Salem," he said, holding out his drawstring to her, "would you tie mine, too?"

Salem tied Raymond Milford's drawstring. And before the day was over she also tied knots for Jeremy O'Bannion, Bobby Troop, Sam Bukowski, and Damon Ross. All of them had the same problem — tying knots; and the same dread — that what happened to Eddie Mott might happen to them. Several of them had already had a nightmare in which Tuna Casseroli was holding them upside down and pantless by the ankles.

A short while later, after practice had begun,

Raymond Milford came running over to Salem on the sideline. His little face was lost in his helmet. His chin didn't stick out far enough to touch his chin strap.

"What is it, Raymond?" said Salem.

"Ah, nothing," said Raymond, his mouth dragging manfully, "just an injury."

"Oh?" Salem looked him over. "Where?"

Raymond looked at her from deep inside his helmet. His eyes grew wide and watery, his lower lip trembled. "My f-f-*finger*!" he bawled, thrusting his hand out to her. "It g-got bent b-b-*back*!"

Salem placed his hand as gently as possible in hers. She inspected the wounded finger, touched it.

"Is it b-*broke*?"

Salem pressed it ever so slightly. "I don't think so. Let's see if it'll bend."

"Do we h-have to?"

"I'll be careful." She pressed on the fingernail and very slowly bent the finger till the tip touched the palm. "There, it's not broken."

Raymond searched her eyes. "But it still *hurrrts*!"

What Salem did then came without thinking, from tearful and tender moments between her and her mother. She lifted the wounded finger to her lips, kissed it, patted it, smiled, and said, "That better?"

Raymond blinked, as if emerging from a dark

room into sunlight. He swallowed a sob, sniffed, looked at his finger. He reached his other hand into his helmet and wiped tears away. He sniffed again, took a deep breath, set his lips, and trotted back onto the field.

Ten minutes later, when Damon Ross came limping off the field with a stubbed toe, Salem said, "Okay, but no kisses."

So it began. And so it happened that as the days passed, bump by bump and ache by pain, Salem Brownmiller became more than a manager.

It happened because of who Salem was, and because of who the 100-pound football team was, which was mostly sixth-graders. It did not take long for these sixth-graders to make a very useful discovery: With Salem they could be themselves in a way that they could not be with Coach Lujak. With Coach Lujak they could not complain. With Coach Lujak they could not admit they were afraid to get tackled or run over. With Coach Lujak they could not show that they didn't care whether they won or lost. With Coach Lujak they could not cry.

With Salem, they could. They did. Salem and her first-aid kit became a healing oasis.

If a kid came to her hurting, she would keep him on the bench and try and fix him. If he didn't get better, he didn't go back into the action, simple as that.

For some players it was a conflict. "But I *have*

to go back!" Jeremy O'Bannion screeched one time, even though he was still obviously sick from the knee he had received in the stomach.

"*Have* to?" scoffed Salem. "What do you mean, *have* to? Look at you. You're sick. You're *green.*"

"It doesn't matter," groaned Jeremy. "You can't be a baby. This is football. If you can't play with a little pain, you should go out for the pattycake team."

Salem raised her eyebrows. "And who says?"

Jeremy nodded toward the field. "You know who."

Salem brought her face practically into Jeremy O'Bannion's helmet. "Is that so? Well, you go tell Coach Lujak that when you're out there on the field, maybe then you belong to him, but when you step over that line" — she pointed to the chalky stripe that marked the sideline — "you're mine. And as long as I'm here, the only thing green on that field is going to be the grass."

Salem could see the relief in Jeremy O'Bannion's face. He argued no more. He simply went behind the bench and gratefully threw up.

Each player learned to use Salem in his own way. Raymond Milford, for example, used her to cry. Almost once a day Raymond showed up in front of Salem, his back to the coach, lip quivering. At first he would fight it. "I c-can't," he would stutter. "Not ag-gain."

Salem would slap him in the shoulder pads. "Oh, hogwash. Sure you can."

"But I'm not even h-hurt. He only h-hollered at me."

"*Hollered* at you? That's even worse. Feelings hurt more than bones. You have to let it out, don't you know that? You boys are so dumb. Listen, you know how you feel better after you throw up?"

Raymond nodded. "Uh-huh."

"Well, crying is like that. Tears are like your feelings throwing up. You'll feel better. Come on now, I'll cry with you. Let it out."

Salem would work up a sniffle, and Raymond would let it out.

With Butchy Wallace, Salem became Sigmund Brownmiller.

"I hate that guy," Butchy would seethe.

"Why is that?" Salem would say calmly.

"He thinks I'm no good."

"Tell me about it."

"He won't let me be the kicker."

"Why not?"

"He says I don't kick it far enough."

"Is he right?"

"No, he's a liar."

"The rat."

"He's stupid."

"He makes a worm look brilliant."

"He stinks."

"I can smell him all the way over here. He smells worse than the droppings of a thousand elephant seals. I'm going to put in an order for gas masks. He's a pollution violation all by himself."

Butchy Wallace would stare at Salem, and sooner or later the fury would drain out of him. He would relax, snap on his chin strap, and trot back onto the field.

Salem personalized her service as much as possible. She tried to meet the needs of every player, every situation. Mark Halley, for example, had a sinus condition, his nose was always running. Mark was one of the few kids in school who carried a handkerchief. But there were no pockets in his football uniform, no place to put a hankie. Salem saw his problem and brought a box of tissues from home.

Then there was Mickey Schultz and his pet horsefly. He brought it to school every day in an old half-pint coleslaw container, with tiny holes poked in the clear plastic lid. Mickey took the horsefly around to classes with him, but he was afraid to leave it unguarded in the locker room during football practice. So for two hours each afternoon, Salem became keeper of the horsefly. It was the biggest thing with wings other than a bird or airplane that she had ever seen. She pitied the poor spider that ever met up with it. She didn't even want to imagine what Mickey Schultz fed it.

Brian Blittman tipped the scales right at the limit of 100 pounds, and he believed that if he ate a mini-box of California raisins halfway through each practice, he would be stronger than the other linemen. Salem was his grocer.

Of course, the first-aid kit was not nearly big enough to hold these extra items, so Salem brought a small suitcase from home. She told Coach Lujak she just needed more room for her first-aid supplies.

Salem saw herself and her sideline as giving the 100-pound warriors a little touch of home during their brief respites from battle. And then one day she brought home out onto the field.

10

It began on a Monday, three days before the first game. In order to give the players a taste of the real thing, Coach Lujak had declared an intra-squad scrimmage. First string against second string. They would play it just like a regular game, from kickoff to final whistle, four quarters long, including time-outs.

Coach Lujak called the first time-out midway through the opening quarter. Salem was sitting at her usual place on the bench, munching on a granola bar, and peering across the football field to where the band was practicing, trying to locate Pickles, when several voices yelled at once: "Manager!"

Salem yipped, "Oh!" She jumped, she lunged for the first-aid kit, she dashed onto the field. What she found were two groups of players standing around, one on either side of the ball, which looked rather ignored and forlorn by itself on the grass. She stopped at the ball, looked at both teams. "Who's hurt?"

Snickers and outright laughter broke out. "Nobody's hurt," said Mr. Lujak. "It's a time-out. You bring out the yellow buckets." He pointed to the sideline. "Yellow buckets."

Salem looked at the sideline. She looked at the coach. "Oh," she said, and wagged her head and chuckled at her own silly mistake. "Sorry, Mr. Lujak. I guess you can tell how many football games I've seen. In fact, I don't think I've ever seen a single one. Come to think of it — wow" — she thought for a second or two — "this is the very first time-out of my entire life. I was never on any kind of team, unless you want to count the spelling team in grade school. I'm not exactly the most coordinated person in the world, as the cheerleaders can tell — "

"Miss Brownmiller!" roared the coach. "The yellow buckets! Now!"

Salem raced to the sideline, knocking her knee three times with the first-aid kit. She limped back with two yellow buckets. Each contained three squeeze-type water bottles with plastic straws, plus several towels. She dropped one bucket off with the first-stringers and one with the second-stringers. That's where she stayed, since Coach Lujak was with the first-stringers.

No one moved.

At last Jeremy O'Bannion spoke up. "Well, come on, Salem."

Salem looked at him. "Come on what?"

"Do your manager thing."

"What's that?"

Several players gave exasperated sighs. "Don't blame her," said Eddie Mott. He pulled a water bottle from the bucket. "Here, do this." He raised the bottle, tipped the straw toward himself, and squeezed. A jet of water streamed into his mouth. He handed her the bottle. "You do it."

Salem raised the bottle, tipped it, squeezed, and watered her own nose.

"No! No!" groaned half the team.

"You do it to *us*," said Jeremy O'Bannion.

"Oh," said Salem.

At which point Coach Lujak blew his whistle, ending the time-out. Eleven second-stringers scowled at Salem. She snatched up the yellow buckets and got out of there before they decided to assassinate her.

By the second time-out, she was ready. So were the second-stringers, having gone unnourished during the first time-out. They stood with their helmets in their hands, their hair plastered with sweat, their mouths open, like eleven guppies waiting to be fed.

Salem flipped two of the bottles to others, kept the third herself and started shooting water. She caught lips and chins on the first few tries, and from then on hit them dead-center in the back of the tongue.

"Towel," called Jeremy O'Bannion.

Salem pulled a towel from the bucket. She offered it to him. He frowned and shook his head. "Face."

Salem blinked, smiled. "Ah!" She mopped his face with the towel, then the ten other faces. When she finished, she felt smiled at and thanked, even though no one came right out and did either. Only Damon Ross spoke, staring pointedly at her, as if delivering a dispatch that she should carry to the home front: "It's murder out here."

The whistle blew: Time-out was over. Salem gathered her goods and returned to the bench, feeling closer than ever to the players and wishing there was more she could do.

By the end of the scrimmage, the two sides had practically plowed each other into the ground. They dragged themselves off the field, muttering things like, "Who needs this?" and "I'm quitting." They threw their helmets down. They spit. They cursed. Five of them lined up to have cuts and scratches tended to.

Bobby Troop had an ugly red, brown, and green skinburn on his arm, the result of a meeting with the first-string fullback and his wall of blockers. He was fighting back tears. "I'm outta here," he told Salem bitterly. "This stinks." Then he screamed aloud as Salem tried to wash the dirt from his wound.

Salem winced, "Oh, I'm sorry, Bobby. I wish I were a better doctor." Her own eyes were welling up.

"It's not your fault," said Raymond Milford, who was next in line. "It's just that we used to play tag football in grade school. Who knew tackle was gonna be like this? The coach thinks we're pros or something. He makes us do everything ten times. He bops us on our helmets. I'm getting a headache."

"We're dog meat," groaned Zachary Riley, flexing his sore knee. "That's all. Dog meat."

"Plus we stink," added John Rankin. "We're gonna lose our first game a hundred to nothing."

The others muttered and nodded.

Salem held up a water-soaked cotton ball. "Hey, wait a minute, that's not true. You guys are *not* dog meat. And you *don't* stink. And you're *not* going to lose a hundred to nothing."

"Right," snickered Zachary Riley. "*Two* hundred to nothing."

"Listen," said Salem, "the first game is Thursday. You can't go into it thinking like that. You have to have a better attitude."

"I gotta have a better *life*," said Zachary Riley. He kicked his helmet ten feet. "I'm quitting."

Salem grabbed his arm. "No!"

Zachary stared at her. "Why not?"

"You don't want to be a quitter, do you?"

"Why not?"

"Then you'll start quitting everything. You'll go through your whole life just giving up every time something gets a little hard."

"A *little* hard?" laughed Zachary. "Why don't *you* go out there and get *your* butt massacred? You sit over here, where it's all safe, eating candy bars. Football used to be easy. It used to be fun. Now it's not. I *hate* it."

"Me, too," said another.

"It wasn't candy," said Salem lamely, "it was a granola bar." She couldn't think of any more arguments, any new way to persuade Zachary and the others not to quit. She had never seen such low morale. How could she, how could anyone, ever change it? "Well, just don't," was all she could say.

Raymond Milford stepped forward. "Why not?" he demanded. "What do we get out of it except beat up, especially us second-stringers? We get the most massacred of all." For once, there were no tears in his eyes.

Salem looked at Raymond, at Zachary, at them all. As a writer, she had always prided herself on her creativity, her imagination. But now, just when she needed it: zero. Her head was as empty as a classroom two seconds after dismissal.

The players began to slump and straggle off to

the locker room. "Wait!" she called. "Don't quit now. Wait till the first game at least. Okay?"

Zachary Riley looked back. "Why should we?"

Salem stomped her foot in frustration. "I don't *know*! Just do it, o-*kay*?"

They did not answer. They resumed their motley plod to the locker room.

And Salem was asking herself, Now, why did I say that?

Salem thought about it all that night and all the next day at school. How could she keep them from quitting? How could she raise their morale? Nothing came to her. She was sure that a true author would never suffer such an appalling lack of ideas. This was worse than the occasional case of writer's block. This was pure brain block, a total eclipse of the mind.

The day was rescued from absolute disaster when, to her great relief, Salem saw Zachary Riley and Raymond Milford and the rest of them heading for the locker room for Tuesday's practice. She tied drawstrings and baby-sat Mickey Schultz's horsefly and did all her other usual duties, then sat on the bench to think some more.

She unwrapped a granola bar and broke off a bite. She gazed about. The cheerleaders were off beyond a set of goalposts, practicing the cheers that she would never lead. As usual, Ms. Baylor was yelling at Sunny: "Smile, Wyler, smile!"

Straight ahead, on the far side of the field beyond the football players, the world's smallest band was marching — or rather bumbling — to the animated directions of the kidney-bean shaped Mr. Hummelsdorf. To Salem's surprise, she noted that Cueball the nickelhead was back, rattling away at his drum and everything else in sight. In fact, the band had grown by two. There were now nine members.

As before, Pickles was the only one who seemed to know what he was doing, marching erect and sure, his arms high, his elbows flared, bugle to his mouth as proudly as if he were in the Rose Bowl Parade. In some strange way, the sounds from his bugle fell upon her as his voice, as notes about to become words.

When Salem's eyes shifted to the football action, she came out of her reverie to find that all but one bite remained of her granola bar. For the first time (other than sleeping) in nearly twenty-four hours, she had not been thinking about the problem of the players. And as often happened — in this case, as she stared at the remaining bite of granola bar in her hand and remembered something Zachary Riley had said — the answer came only when she stopped looking for it.

11

Thursday was a day of surprises for Eddie Mott.

His first surprise was finding himself named as starting free safety for the Fighting Hamsters' opening game against Tarrytown Middle School. Eddie wasn't kidding himself; he knew he wasn't that great a player. And he knew the reason for his promotion from second string was that the usual starting safety, Ned Povich, had cracked a finger against somebody's helmet and was out for the season.

Still, Eddie was determined to make the most of his opportunity. If only he could get lucky, he thought, intercept a pass and return it for a long touchdown, maybe everybody would forget about the underwear business. Maybe they would stop calling him "Supe" in the hallways. Maybe Tuna Casseroli would stop pointing to him from the varsity practice area and laughing and raising his hands as if holding someone upside down by the ankles.

Eddie was told about his starting role by Coach Lujak in the locker room before the game. He got his second surprise as he trotted out to the field with the team. The Hamster Band was there, marching off a last-minute rehearsal for their half-time show, and Eddie was flabbergasted to see that the drummer was none other than the crazy nickelhead, Cueball. In fact, there were two other nickelheads in the band. One played a soda bottle, blowing across the mouth to produce a breathy, mournful sound; the other played a kazoo.

Eddie was not aware of why this had come about. He did not know that after the shouting match in the parking lot that day, Lips Hummelsdorf had had second thoughts about kicking Cueball off the band. The problem was numbers. Now that he had committed himself to fielding the county's only middle school football marching band — and very likely the world's smallest — he calculated that he needed at least ten members to make it work.

Why?

The letter P. What good was a marching band if it could not form the school's initials on the playing field during the halftime show? Michigan State University, for example, Lips' college alma mater, formed a colossal MSU that went practically from sideline to sideline, goalpost to goalpost. Of course, they had 200 members, as did many college bands. Easy for them. Even Cedar

Grove High School had enough members to make a respectable CGHS on the field.

Hummelsdorf knew that a three-letter formation — P(lumstead) M(iddle) S(chool) — was out of the question. The best he could hope for was a P for Plumstead. But after banishing the crazed nickelhead, he was left with four short of the ten people necessary to form a readable P.

And so, despite the lunatic drummer's insubordination, when he came around the next day whining to be let back in the band, Hummelsdorf swallowed his pride and said okay. On one condition: if the kid brought along three more band members. Well, he came up with two — fellow nickelheads, it turned out — bringing the count to nine. And on Thursday morning, with the first football game mere hours away, Hummelsdorf came to the decision that he had hoped he would never have to make: He himself would become the tenth Marching Hamster. He himself would complete the Plumstead P.

Eddie Mott, of course, did not know all this. All he knew was that a nickelhead had dared call Mr. Hummelsdorf "Lips" to his face and not only lived to see the next day, but was readmitted to the band — along with two more nickelheads! Was there nothing these guys couldn't get away with?

Before the game Salem came over to him. She smiled. "Nervous?"

"Nah," he answered as casually as he could.

"Want me to tighten those pants some more?"

"Nah." He knew what she was thinking. It was bad enough for his pants to fall down during practice, but for them to drop in front of the bleachers full of students, teachers, parents . . . He shrugged. "Well, okay, if you insist, go ahead."

Salem gave the drawstring a double knot. She was grinning.

"What's so funny?"

"Oh," she said, giving the knot a final tug, "I was just wondering why you never let me do anything but this."

Eddie stepped back and adjusted his hip pads. "What do you mean?"

"I mean you never ask me to help you, like the other guys. There's nothing in my suitcase for you. I saw you get hurt a couple of times in practice, but you didn't even come over to get first aid."

Eddie looked around. The Tarrytown team was warming up across the way. "I got a game to play," he said. "Ask me later."

She grabbed his chin strap. "I'm asking now."

He glared at her, took in a whistling breath. "Look, you want to baby those guys, that's your business."

"They seem to like it," she said.

"Fine. That's their business. That doesn't mean I have to like it."

She flicked the tip of his nose with the chin

strap. She was enjoying this. "Don't you know I'm your mother out here on the football field? Mr. Lujak is your father, and I'm your mama."

He slapped her hand from his chin strap. "Not *my* mother, you're not. I got one mother, that's enough. That's the reason I came out for football. I'm trying to get away from mothers, so I can grow up. This is football, y'know, not pattycake." He walked off.

"Well ex-*cuuuze* me," said Salem, pretending to be huffy. Then she called, "Eddie!"

He stopped but did not turn. "See you at the first time-out!" he heard her sing.

Whatever that meant. Eddie had more important things on his mind, like Tarrytown. He joined the other players for a final huddle with Coach Lujak, who told the players this was what they had all been working and sacrificing for. Now it was time to show what they were made of. Time to toughen up! Time to kick some tail! Time to go down in history! Time to give Plumstead Middle School its first-ever victory in sports!

"Yeah!" shouted Eddie, piling his hands onto the others in the huddle. He raced onto the field, yelling and pumping his fists, ready to kill. Then he discovered his mistake. Plumstead was receiving the kickoff, meaning they would be on offense. He was a defensive player; he didn't belong on the field. He ran off.

The Fighting Hamsters failed to make a first

down and had to punt to Tarrytown. Eddie and his defensive mates took the field. As free safety, Eddie was the farthest back from the line of scrimmage, the last line of defense, the last hope. If a Tarrytown player managed to get through all ten of the other Hamsters, it was Eddie's job to stop him. There was nothing behind Eddie but the goal line.

As he waited for the play to begin, he heard a voice: "Hey, Supe!" The voice was coming from a bunch of varsity players, heading for practice on another field. He saw an upraised hand, a flash of red. Tuna Casseroli was waving a pair of Superman undershorts in the air and laughing and pointing. "Hey, Supe! Hey, Supe!"

Eddie turned away. "I'll show ya," he said through gritted teeth, "I'll show ya."

Tarrytown ran its first play and — oh, no! — it was Eddie's worst nightmare. The Tarrytown line opened a hole big enough for an elephant. The Tarrytown fullback charged through and into the Hamster backfield. He stiff-armed Damon Ross, ran right past Sam Bukowski, and steamrollered over Zachary Riley as if he were no more than a dandelion — and now he was heading Eddie's way. Eddie planted his feet wide, crouched, ready to go left or right, but one look at the frightening sneer on this guy's face and Eddie knew he wasn't going anywhere but straight ahead. Eddie froze. The last he saw of the fullback was the sneer —

he could even smell his breath — and then Eddie was flying, and then he was on his back looking up at a dinosaur-shaped cloud in the sky, and then the rest of the Tarrytown team was stampeding over him on their way to mobbing the fullback in the end zone.

The extra point was good. Tarrytown 7, Plumstead 0.

When Eddie got back to the bench, Jeremy O'Bannion pointed to Eddie's chest and said, "Hey, look!"

Eddie looked. Stamped across the 8 of his number 89 was the perfect footprint of the Tarrytown fullback. Eddie groaned and slumped onto the bench. But not for long. Within a minute Tarrytown had the ball again, and he had to go back out on defense.

This time it took Tarrytown three plays to score. And this time Eddie never even touched the fullback, as he was obliterated by a pair of blockers.

Tarrytown 14, Plumstead 0.

When Tarrytown threatened to score again a few minutes later, Coach Lujak called from the sideline: "Time-out!"

All the Hamsters but Eddie took off their helmets and flopped to the ground. "Come on," Eddie told them. "Don't let them see you like that. We gotta be tough."

"*You* be tough, " said Zachary Riley. "I'm not

even waiting till after the game. I'm quitting at halftime."

"Who's waiting till halftime?" said Mickey Schultz, lifting himself painfully to his feet. "I'm taking my fly and going home now, while I'm still alive."

As Mickey Schultz turned to walk off, he bumped into Salem, who said, "Where are you going?"

"Home, to play pattycake."

Salem grinned. She had her usual yellow time-out bucket with her, but she also had a suitcase, a different one than before. It was old and beat up, but it was a lot bigger, and painted on its side in tall white and purple letters were the words FIGHTING HAMSTERS. "You'll be sorry," she sang.

From the gleam in her eye and the tone of her voice, Mickey Schultz could tell she was right. So he stayed.

Salem stepped in among the eleven players and set down the suitcase. "Hamsters," she said brightly, "behold — the dawn of a new age in time-outs."

She opened the suitcase, laid its two sides flat on the ground. Twenty-two eyelids shot up like tiny shades. Twenty-two eyes gaped in wonder at what they saw.

12

There were chocolate-chip cookies. There were graham cracker, chocolate, and marshmallow s'mores. There were Rice Krispies squares and chocolate-covered pretzels and peanut-butter fudge and chocolate-walnut brownies and cupcakes with icing and candy beads and bite-size squares of Sicilian pizza, some with a pepperoni circle, some with a mushroom.

Salem pulled the straw-top plastic bottles from the yellow bucket. It wasn't water in them. "Hawaiian Punch," she said.

She picked up a round chocolate-cake sandwich with white cream in the middle. She held it out to Mickey Shultz. "Guess what this is called?"

"Pattycake!" exclaimed Mickey and snatched it from her hand.

The team attacked the suitcase — except for Eddie Mott.

"C'mon," said Salem, "don't be such a pooper.

You're missing the world's first gourmet time-out."

Eddie growled at her. "You're just making a joke out of everything. This doesn't have anything to do with football."

Salem moved closer to Eddie. She whispered, "It does if it keeps them from quitting the team. Now stop being such a jerk. Eat."

Eddie just glared at her as the official blew the whistle, ending the time-out. Salem closed the suitcase, nearly snipping off a few lingering fingers. Mickey Shultz quickly jammed a cookie into his pants. Zachary Riley stuffed a s'more into his shoulder pads. As the players pulled on their helmets, their cheeks bulged like chipmunks'.

Salem glanced back with a flirtatious wave. "See ya next time-out, *boyzzzz*."

Nothing about the football game changed. Tarrytown scored a third touchdown two plays later. They continued to score at will.

The difference was, none of the Fighting Hamsters, except Eddie Mott, was very upset about it. They were thinking more about the next time-out than the next tackle. Their problem was no longer the Tarrytown team, but how to eat and play football at the same time.

On the play after the first time-out, for example, Mickey Schultz took a body block that crushed his cookie. For the rest of the half, Coach Lujak believed Mickey was especially lively on his toes, dancing this way and that to make blockers miss him. The truth was that the chocolate-chip cookie crumbs in Mickey's pants were driving him crazy.

Then there was Sam Bukowski. Sam had pigged out more than anyone else during the first time-out. In less than two minutes he was seen to wolf down three cupcakes, five chocolate-covered pretzels, two brownies, and half a bottle of Hawaiian Punch. Then, as Salem was closing the suitcase, he grabbed a handful of bite-size Sicilian pizza squares, which he dumped into his helmet before pulling it on.

Within minutes, Sam became very sluggish. He dropped into his crouch on the line of scrimmage and never really rose out of it. He was involved in plays only if by accident they happened to come straight at him. On those occasions, the slightest bump was enough to send him reeling onto his rump. At one point during the action, one of the pizza squares slid down and began to ooze red and cheesy through the ear hole of his helmet, causing the Tarrytown player who had just blocked him to cry out in horror: "I just knocked his brains out!"

The Tarrytown player fainted and had to be revived and helped from the field. As for Sam Bukowski, the referee discovered what was really protruding from the helmet hole and ejected Sam from the game.

Sam refused to go.

The referee's eyes boggled. He seethed. He blew his whistle, called an officials' time-out, pointed to the Plumstead bench, and commanded: "Out!"

"No, please!" begged Sam. "I'll be good from now on! Look — " He took off his helmet and dumped the remaining pizza squares to the ground. "See, they're gone."

"Out!" roared the referee.

Sam fell to his knees. "No! Please don't kick me out!"

In all his career as a football official, the referee had never come across a player who refused to be kicked out of a game. Spitting out his whistle, he took three strides toward the Hamster bench and yelled: "If somebody doesn't come out here and remove this player from the field, this game will be over and declared a forfeit to the visiting team!"

Coach Lujak himself then ran onto the field, as did Salem. As Sam was dragged from the field, he kept looking back at the huddle of his teammates and the suitcase unfolding. "No, Coach," he kept crying, "let me play! I love football!"

With a minute to go in the first half, Tarrytown scored its seventh touchdown for a 44 to 0 lead. The Plumstead offense took their positions on the field to receive the kickoff. They were a happier bunch than when they had started the game. They had had three of the most wonderful and delicious time-outs in the history of football, and looked forward to an equally tasty second half.

As the two teams spread out across the field, awaiting the referee's whistle, they could not have looked more different. The Tarrytown players were clenched and snarling, anxious as horses in the starting gate, hungry for more points, eager to wrest the ball from Plumstead and score yet again.

The Hamsters, on the other hand, were a picture of contentment. Life had suddenly become very good to them. From their side of the field came languid smiles and the gentle sounds of burping and stomachs gurgling.

In the meantime, the Fighting Hamsters marching band had come down from the bleachers and lined up in the end zone behind the Hamster players. Director Hummelsdorf thought he remembered it being done this way from his days at Michigan State. Beyond that, however, he was strictly guessing. Hummelsdorf knew about tubas and flutes and any other instrument you could name, but he didn't know a thing about football.

The referee raised his whistle to his lips. In that moment before the kickoff, the field was quiet, the sidelines were quiet. The bleachers were not. There was a commotion, shouting. Distracted, the referee took the whistle from his mouth and turned to see what the problem was.

13

What the referee saw was a Plumstead cheer-leader, in her white sweater and purple-and-white pleated skirt, pointing to the bleachers and yelling loudly enough to be heard from one end of the field to the other: "That's it, nickelnose! If you're gonna sit in front of me, you're gonna cheer!"

"I'll cheer when I feel like it!" the spectator with a strange haircut yelled back. "It's a free country!"

"Love it or leave it, polka-dot head! I'm not here for my health! You cheer or you clear out!"

"I'll cheer when you start smiling, you grouch-bag! Who ever heard of a cheerleader who don't smile?"

"You wanna come on down here and make me, butt-face?"

"Yeah, yeah, I'll come down and make ya!"

As Sunny Wyler stood squarely before the bleachers, as the spectators gaped in amazement, the nickelhead came down, stopped on the front row, leaned down, thrust the forefingers of each hand into the sides of Sunny's mouth, and pulled upward and outward.

"Have a nice d — " the nickelhead managed to get out before Sunny slapped his nose sideways. The nickelhead yelped and took off behind the bleachers, Sunny lit out after him, and the referee returned his attention to the game. He blew the whistle.

At the sound of the whistle two things happened: (1) the Tarrytown kicker began running toward the ball; (2) Lips Hummelsdorf blew *his* whistle, and the Fighting Hamster band began marching forward. Only one of these things was supposed to happen.

Director Hummelsdorf, unacquainted with football as he was, thought the referee's whistle meant the end of the first half, so he in turn ordered his troops forward. As the ball left the foot of the Tarrytown kicker, the band moved from the end zone onto the field.

The ball sailed end over end to the twenty-yard line, where it was caught — to everyone's surprise — by Sam Bukowski. Still stuffed and woozy but determined not to miss any more time-outs, Sam had sneaked onto the field with the offense. That made him the twelfth player on an eleven-member side, but no one was counting.

Sam made the mistake of catching the ball more

with his stomach than with his hands. He took two running steps, stopped, said, "Uh-oh," and dropped the ball.

"Fumble!" yelled the oncharging Tarrytown players. Three of them dove for it just as Sam barfed, coating the ball with a warm Sicilian pizza and chocolate-chip soup.

The ball, quite slippery now, squirted from the grasp of the three Tarrytown players, who then began screaming and clawing madly at the grass. Players from both teams — at least, those who did not yet realize that the ball was covered by more than pigskin — picked up the chase. A player from Plumstead would scoop up the ball, discover what he had in his hands, scream, and fling the ball away. A Tarrytown player would then scoop it up and go through the same thing.

Meanwhile, the band was up to the forty-yard line, only to find themselves surrounded by players darting this way and that after the bounding ball. Seeing that it would be just as difficult to retreat as to press on, Director Hummelsdorf thrust his baton forward and commanded, "Onward, Hamsters!" Flying football bodies took their toll on the band. The flutist fell at the forty-five-yard line, the triangle player at the fifty; but the band, led by the blare of Pickles' bugle and the rattle of Cueball's drum, marched on.

By now, half of the twenty-two players on the field were screaming and clawing at the grass. The

81

remaining players, fully understanding the situation, had no intention of touching the contaminated ball — at least, not with their hands. So they began to kick it, and suddenly the game looked more like soccer than football.

At first the players kicked aimlessly at the ball. Then it seemed to dawn on all of them at once: The thing to do was kick the ball all the way into the other team's end zone, then, somehow, pick it up and thus score a touchdown.

In the meantime the zebra-shirted officials were trying to wave the band off the field while whipping out their rule books to see if interference by barf or bands was covered. The referee, eyes on stopwatch, blew his whistle when time expired — not that it made any difference, for the play in progress had to be allowed to run its course.

The officials waved, the band marched, the "soccer" game played on, and Sam Bukowski, feeling better now but awfully tired, lay down and went to sleep between the twenty-five- and thirty-yard lines. A thundering kick by a Tarrytown player sent the ball sailing toward the Plumstead goal. It landed on the twenty-yard line and rolled into the end zone and sat there, a touchdown prize for the first Tarrytown player to reach it.

A Tarrytown linebacker, from forty yards away, began a dead sprint for the ball at the same time that Sunny Wyler's nickelhead came tearing back around the bleachers with Sunny on his tail.

Screeching and flapping his arms like a goose taking off, the nickelhead circled the field down to the Plumstead end, veered sharply, and headed onto the field itself. He dashed under the goalposts, through the end zone, and collided at the goal line with the Tarrytown linebacker just as he was about to reach for the ball.

As the nickelhead and the linebacker lay dazed on the field, the next player on the scene happened to be Eddie Mott. All this time Eddie had been planning what to do if he ever got near the barfed-on ball. Now was his chance. He yanked off his helmet and stuffed it like a sleeve down over the ball till only the tip of the ball was sticking out. Holding the helmet by an ear hole, he began running in the opposite direction. He ran past the band, he ran past the officials, he ran past the players on both sides. He ran 103 yards, all the way to the Tarrytown goal line. He stood in the Tarrytown end zone, jumping and yelling and waving his helmet.

The referee came running. He saw, he thrust his arms to the sky: Touchdown!

The first half was over.

14

There was plenty to talk about on the picklebus ride home that night. The two headliners were Eddie and Sunny: Eddie because he had scored the Hamsters' only touchdown in Plumstead's 84-to-6 loss to Tarrytown, and Sunny because she had been kicked off the cheerleading squad for attacking a fan.

"That's what Ms. Baylor called him," snorted Sunny. "A fan. He's no fan. If he was a fan, he would've been cheering. He's a jerk."

"He's a hero, too," said Salem. "Everybody's saying if it wasn't for him crashing into the Tarrytown guy, they would have scored the touchdown and we would have had zero."

"And Crazylegs Mott never would have had a chance to be a hero himself," added Pickles as he guided the green bus the long way home to give them more time to talk. "Who would have ever thought it — Eddie Mott has something to thank a nickelhead for."

"So I guess I should thank Sunny then, too," said Eddie, who rode the third slot between Salem and Sunny. "If she didn't chase the nickelhead, he never would've crashed into the Tarrytown kid."

"He's lucky he crashed into the kid," said Sunny. "If I caught him he wouldn't have got off so easy."

The four pickleteers laughed. The bus rolled on.

"I warned you," Salem called back good-naturedly. "You can't be a grouch and a cheerleader at the same time."

"So what are you going to be now?" said Pickles. "A hit girl? Carry a club to each game, bop everybody on the head who doesn't cheer?"

More laughter.

When quiet returned, Sunny said, "I already know what I'm going to be."

Three heads turned, waiting.

"I'm going to be the mascot."

"We already have Humphrey," said Eddie, referring to the school's pet hamster and the inspiration for the football team's nickname.

"Humphrey can't come to the games," Sunny pointed out. "And even if I brought him, he wouldn't do any good. He's too little. Nobody would take him seriously. What this joint needs is a *big* hamster to whip these people into shape."

"Nobody says a hamster has to smile, right, Sunshine?"

"Right," said Sunny, who allowed only these three friends and the principal, Mr. Brimlow, to call her by her given name.

"Nobody says a hamster has to be nice."

"Exactly."

"Don't you need permission?"

"From who?" said Sunny. "Mr. Brimlow? He won't care. This is school spirit. Who's gonna say no to that?"

"The nickelheads?" suggested Pickles.

"Wanna bet?" said Sunny.

Nobody took the bet.

Pickles held up his hand. "First stop coming up — Brrrrownmiller rrrresidence."

"Oh, no," Salem protested. "It's too soon. Go around the block once."

"I have homework," said Pickles.

"I have dinner," said Sunny.

Salem climbed off with a groan and sulked away. Suddenly she brightened, she turned. "Hey — if we can't go around the block, let's have a party. My house. Saturday. What do you say?"

"Don't go," said Eddie. "I was at her house once, and she made me drink this punch from hell, and I was sick all the next day."

"It was Periwinkle Punch," sniffed Salem haughtily, "and this child made himself ill by eating everything in sight."

"I'll be there," said Pickles. "I'll drag the Mottster along."

"Me, too," said Sunny.

Salem clapped her hands. "Good! Once I get you there, I'm going to convince you all to come to the Halloween dance with me. See ya." She dashed into her house.

Pickles called, "Next stop, the Wyler rrrresidence."

Eddie said nothing all the way to Sunny's house. He just concentrated on knowing that she was mere inches behind him on the picklebus.

Pickles left off Sunny and headed for Eddie's.

"Did you ever stop and think about what you did today?" said Pickles.

"Sure," said Eddie, "I scored a TD. A hundred and three yards long."

"Right, but it was more than just that, you know."

"What do you mean?"

"It was a first, Motto. That's what makes it really special. Look, who was the fourteenth president?"

"I don't know."

"Who was the first?"

"George Washington."

"Who was the first man to walk on the moon?"

"Michael Jackson."

Pickles threw up his hands. "No, no, Mottster. Michael Jackson was the first to *do* the Moon*walk*. Neil Armstrong was the first to *walk* on the *moon*."

"Right," said Eddie. "I knew that."

"So, who was the second man to walk on the moon?"

"Michael Jordan." Pickles groaned and looked back at his passenger. "Just kidding," said Eddie. "Actually, I don't know."

"Neither do I," said Pickles. "See, that's what I mean. Nobody knows who was second or third or seventy-seventh. Just the first, that's who everybody remembers. That's what goes down in the history books."

Eddie gasped. *"History* books?"

"Sure. When somebody does something for the first time, it's historic."

"Wow," went Eddie. He tried the word himself. *"Historic."* His shoulders tingled.

"That's how it is with first things," said Pickles, pulling up to Eddie's house. Eddie stepped from the bus. "Look at it this way — if Plumstead lasts for a thousand years and the hundred-pound football teams score a million touchdowns, even if the universe lasts forever, there can only ever be one first touchdown scored at Plumstead Middle School, and — "

Pickles handed the rest of the sentence over to Eddie. Eddie finished it in a dry, awestruck whisper: " — and I scored it."

Pickles saluted him. "Bingo. And not only that. You're probably the first person — shoot, you're probably the *only* person — ever to score a touchdown by carrying the ball in his helmet, in the history of *football*, period." He thumped Eddie's shoulder. "Think about it."

The two shared a reverent minute of silence at the very thought of it.

"Well," said Pickles at last, "gotta go. See ya at the flagpole." Pickles and Eddie, by appointment of Principal Brimlow, had the job of raising the flag at the school every morning.

"See ya," Eddie answered absently and went inside.

That evening Eddie had trouble concentrating — on dinner, on taking a bath, on homework. What Pickles had said kept replaying in his head, especially the word "*historic . . . historic.*" Instead of focusing on his division problems, he kept imagining a history book of the future. In his mind he flipped the pages . . . here was George Washington crossing the Delaware . . . here was Neil Armstrong stepping off the ladder of the lunar module onto the dusty surface of the moon . . . here was Edward A. Mott, scoring the first touchdown for Plumstead Middle School. Washington. Armstrong. Mott. He got the chills.

He imagined that one day there would be a monument at the football field, perhaps just beyond the goalposts where he began his historic 103-yard run. Perhaps the monument would be a tall, diamond-tipped obelisk, like the Washington Monument. Or maybe it would be a statue, showing him running, helmet in hand, the tip of the ball barely sticking out.

He imagined, years from now, his teammates bringing their children to the field, showing them the monument and saying, "Yes, Junior, it's true. I knew Eddie Mott personally. We played on the very same team together. I was here that day. Saw it with my own eyes. I can tell you, it was an honor just to be there. He was the greatest player I've ever seen. He was truly historic."

Maybe then the old teammates would take their kids inside the school, to the trophy case. They would stand there silently, respectfully, looking at the jersey. "That's his, all right," an old teammate would say, wiping away a tear of remembrance, "ol' number eighty-nine."

When Eddie finally got to sleep that night, he was thinking about how great it was to be finally rid of that Superman underwear stigma. He was thinking of what to say to the reporters and TV crews who were bound to be waiting when he showed up at the flagpole the next day. He was wondering whether to give Neil Armstrong a call.

15

Riding to school the next day, Salem could not have been more pleased with herself. She had succeeded beyond her own hopes, which had been simply to keep morale high enough so the players wouldn't quit. Well, not only were the players staying, they had to be the happiest team in all of football. Chattering, laughing, cheering. By the end of the game, their morale had been so high — their only complaint was that the game was over — you would have sworn they had just won 84 to 6, not lost. And then to see them charging at her, sweeping her and her magic suitcase onto their padded shoulders, giving her the ride of her life across the field and into the school, begging her to be their manager forever — it was all she could do to keep from breaking down and bawling like a baby, she was so happy.

Of course, there was the little matter of the coach. After looking up to see her riding the shoulders of the team, he babbled something about "hopeless pattycakers" and announced that as of that moment he was quitting. He stomped off to his car and drove away. Nobody begged him to stay.

Right then everyone began wondering who the next coach would be. Some suggested it should be Salem. Salem laughed it off and told them she was having too much fun being student manager. Besides, she didn't consider getting a new coach a problem. From what she had seen of football, practically anybody could coach it. It was a simple enough game, especially if you were properly fed.

These happy thoughts were on her mind as she got off her bus in the school driveway. Normally, she would not have noticed the flagpole, but today, with kids looking up and laughing, she followed the pointing fingers to the top. Her first impression was of a flash of red and blue; she thought that odd, since Eddie and Pickles didn't usually raise the flag till everyone was in homeroom.

Then, shielding her eyes from the sun glare, she saw that it was not the flag at all, but underwear — red-and-blue Superman underwear — hanging from the top! Salem's heart sank. Oh, no, she thought, she ached, poor Eddie!

Pickles was running out then, running out with his bugle and the triangle-folded American flag under his arm, pushing through the giggling gawkers to the pole. Salem rushed over. "Let me help," she said, taking the flag and bugle. In a blur Pickles unwrapped the ropes from the metal cleat and — *zing!* — pulled the underwear down so fast it seemed weighted with lead. Pickles fastened the real flag to the rope, raised it so that it came blooming red, white, and blue out of Salem's hands, then gave her one rope and said, "Pull slow." As she did so, he raised the ancient, dented bugle to his lips and, as he did every morning, played reveille.

By the time the flag reached the top, the crowd of kids was hushed. Then they applauded and whistled while Pickles and Salem went into the school. Pickles stuffed the underwear into his pocket.

"Did he see it?" said Salem.

Pickles nodded grimly. "Yeah. He took off. I don't know where he is."

Salem sniffled, "He felt so good yesterday, so proud of himself. I thought this was all over."

"So did I."

They both looked down the long hallway, at the kids draining into their homerooms.

It was midway through third period when Mrs. Oates, the home skills teacher, brought the bald young man into the principal's office. She was decidedly nervous and no doubt relieved to be handing the boy over.

"I found him in my supply closet," she said. "I almost stepped on him. He was just sitting there on the floor. Almost scared me to death." She glared at the boy, retasting her anger. She gave the principal a hopeless look, shrugged. "Won't tell me his name. Won't speak."

The principal nodded. "Okay, thank you. I'll see to it."

"Hair all over the floor of the closet."

"Mm."

"Guess I'll get stuck with cleaning it up."

The principal's eyes shifted toward the door. The home skills teacher left.

Mr. Brimlow smiled. "How are you doing, Eddie?" He got up, pointed to the two high-backed leather chairs on the other side of the office. "Have a seat." In certain situations he made a point of getting out from behind the desk, where the appearance was Me Big Authority Figure, You Little Student Nobody.

The boy was still standing. Mr. Brimlow sat. "Eddie, come on." Eddie sat.

Mr. Brimlow had arrived at school well before the first bus, as usual, and had not noticed the flagpole. Only later, from his office window, did he hear and witness the episode. He was proud of the way Pickles and Salem handled things. He was especially sensitive to anything involving his Principal's Posse. And now he hurt for Eddie Mott.

Seeing Eddie in the high-backed chair reminded Mr. Brimlow of the first time he had ever laid eyes on him. It was the first day of school, and his first job as principal had been to coax this frightened sixth-grader from the back of the school bus. He didn't want to come out because some eighth-graders had tossed him around on the way to school. And now this.

He decided not to meet the issue head-on. Not an easy job, considering the sight before him. Eddie's scalp was not bald in the strictest sense. At its shortest, it was about a quarter-inch long. Here and there brown tufts cropped up. It looked ragged, more chewed than cut, as if he had been locked in that closet with a hungry goat. Add to that the most sad-sack face Mr. Brimlow had ever seen, and the principal managed to keep a straight face only because of equal pressure to both laugh and cry.

"So, Eddie," he said as casually as possible, "I hear you really did a number on that Tarrytown team yesterday. People are still talking about that touchdown you scored."

"I want to go to Alaska," Eddie muttered in a monotone.

The principal tried to keep his eyes planted on the boy's face, not his Charlie Brown dome. "Why Alaska, Eddie?"

"They hate me here. I cut my hair. I can't go home. I can't face anybody. I want to go to Alaska."

Mr. Brimlow took a deep breath. He needed

help. He looked at his watch. "Tell you what," he said, "you just sit here for a little while. This isn't our usual Posse lunch day, but maybe we'll call a special session."

Mr. Brimlow went to the outer office and gave directions to the secretary, Mrs. Wilburham. Not long after, as the bell rang for lunch, the other three Posse members walked into the office.

"Eek," went Sunny when she saw Eddie.

"Oh," went Salem.

Pickles said nothing.

Salem went right over and sat on the arm of Eddie's chair.

Sunny just stood there.

Pickles turned to the principal. "I think you'd better let us handle this."

The principal thought for a moment, nodded, and left the office. He heard the door close behind him.

Ten minutes later Pickles came out, walked briskly through the outer office, and down the hallway. He came back with a roll of gauze, white tape, and scissors.

After another ten minutes Brimlow heard laughter on the other side of the office door.

When the bell rang to end lunch, the four of them emerged chattering and in every other way normal, except for the bandage bowl that capped Eddie's head. The principal and the secretary just stood there staring as the sixth-graders breezed on by. Pickles gave a thumbs-up sign, Salem whispered in passing, "Tell you about it later," and they were gone.

Knowing how much Salem loved to talk, Mr. Brimlow was confident she would keep her word. Sure enough, within seconds after last bell, she was standing before his desk, huffing, glancing at the clock. "Okay, Mr. Brimlow (huff, huff). Only have a minute. Have to get to foot (huff) ball practice. First of all (gulp), you know Eddie, *always* overreacting, right? Well, we can't change that. His personality's set, probably for life. He's an overreactor. So (sigh) we're just — 'we're' meaning Sunny, Pickles, and I — we're just going to have to be around to clean up the messes he makes of his life, right? . . . Right?"

She expected an answer.

"Yes, right."

"Right. So, here's what we did. Two-part plan. Part one — Pickles' idea — bandage his head and make it look like he got injured in the football game yesterday. That's what we'll tell people. What this will do is, capital A under part one, it will hide what he did to his hair, in school, anyway. We can't stop the grief he's going to get at home. Capital B, it will get him some sympathy from the other kids. And capital C, it will draw their attention away from his underwear, which, personally, is what I think he was trying to do subconsciously when he cut his hair in the first place."

She took a deep breath, glanced at the clock. "Gotta go. Part two, quick. My idea. I told myself we have to give him something to live for, some-thing to make him happy. What could that *be*? I asked myself. Then it came to me. I whispered it to him so no one else could hear, and presto!" — she snapped her fingers — "he was cured." She looked at the clock. "Yikes! Gotta go."

She started off. Mr. Brimlow grabbed her by the book bag. "Hey, you can't leave me hanging like that."

She stared up at him, blinking, thinking, in a rare reluctance to speak. She gave a sheepish smile. "Well, it's sort of personal."

He released her book bag. He said nothing more, demanded no more information, knowing full well it was not in her power to keep her mouth shut.

Again she glanced at the clock. Then glanced around. She moved in close to him, did not look up, whispered to his chest: "I'm having a party tomorrow. I told him I'd fix it so he could kiss Sunny." She ran. " 'Bye!"

16

"Forget it," said Sunny. "No way. *Nada.* N-O-P-E."

"Oh, Sunny," said Salem. "don't be such a poop."

"If I want to be a poop, I'll be a poop."

"It's not going to kill you."

"Oh, really? So that means I should do it? Just 'cause I'm not gonna die?"

"The *point* is, you don't have to *do* anything. All you have to do is let *him* kiss *you.*"

"No."

"Sunny, it's a good cause."

"So's Save the Whales. I'll give to that. I'll let a whale kiss me."

"Sunny, I promised."

"Fine. Then let him kiss you."

Salem shook her fist at the ceiling. "Ouuu . . . you are incorrigible."

"Don't curse at me," said Sunny. "And besides, you lied. You told me to come early to help you get ready for the party, and all you're doing is telling me I should let some bald-headed kid who thinks he's Superman put his lips on me. Some friend you turned out to be."

Salem sighed mightily. "He is not bald. He does not think he is Superman. He burned his Superman underwear. All he is is a person who was really feeling rotten, and here you have a chance to make him feel really good. You can turn his whole life around. It's in your power. And it's not like he's some stranger, you know. He's the person who pulled you out of the tire when the picklebus crashed. He's our friend. He's *your* friend."

Sunny crunched a potato chip. "He's also a boy." She crunched another chip. She almost grinned. "Anyway, I know what you're really up to."

Salem's eyebrows arched. "Do tell? And what might that be, if I may ask?"

Sunny reached for another chip. "I've seen you look at Pickles. You just want to get something started so you can lay a wet one on him."

Salem was dumbstruck. She stared speechless at Sunny for a painfully long time, listening to Sunny chew chip after chip but hearing the crunching of her own private life. Then came the merciful sound of the doorbell. "It's them," she said and opened the door for Pickles and Eddie.

Pickles was carrying a plastic bag. "What's that?" said Salem.

"You'll see," said Pickles. He handed the bag

to Sunny. "A little present for you."

Sunny pulled a mask from the bag. She frowned at it. "Huh?"

"It's a hamster," said Pickles. "Didn't you say you were going to be a hamster at the football games from now on? So, here's your hamster face." He took the mask from her. "See, it used to be Bugs Bunny. I made it for Halloween a couple years ago. Eddie helped me. We clipped off the ears, painted the face light brown, like Humphrey. We kept the whiskers." He turned it to Salem. "What do you think it looks like?"

Salem threw up her arms. "Why, it's a *hamster*!"

Pickles put the mask over Sunny's head. She looked at herself in the mirror. "I'm working on the rest of the costume," said Pickles. "It should be ready by next game."

The hamster head nodded. "Okay, but it still looks half-rabbit to me."

"No problem," said Pickles. "Call it a ramster."

"When do we eat?" said Eddie, now wearing a baseball cap instead of a bandage.

"*Maintenant*," said Salem.

"Huh?"

"That means 'now' in French." Salem ushered them into the dining room.

"Wow," said Pickles.

"Double wow," said Eddie.

The table had been exquisitely set by Salem, to

whom every event was an occasion. There was a sky-blue tablecloth, and contrasting pure white porcelain dishware, and fine, fancy silverware. There were eight white bowls containing the following: strawberries, pineapple chunks, banana slices, potato chips, pretzels, pound-cake squares, vanilla wafers, and pieces of peanut-butter granola bars.

In the center of the table were two larger items. One was a clear crystal bowl, huge and half-filled with a pink punch in which floated an iceberg of sherbet. The other item was a metal, copper-colored pan, resting several inches above the tablecloth on a wiry base. In the center of the base sat a short, fat candle throwing a blue flame onto the underside of the copper pan.

"Is that what I think it is?" said Eddie, staring straight down into the pan.

Salem nodded. "Behold, *le chocolat*."

"Melted?"

"And warm."

"To *drink*?"

Salem sighed. "To dip. It's fondue."

"Great!" exclaimed Eddie, and immediately dipped his right forefinger into the warm, liquidy chocolate.

If Salem had not screamed, Eddie might not have flinched, and a drop of chocolate might not have flown from his finger onto the sky-blue tablecloth. But Salem did scream and Eddie did flinch, and now she ran to the kitchen and returned with a dishcloth and started scrubbing frantically at the dark-brown spot, muttering, "Cold water. Cold water takes out stains, if you get it soon enough. If. If. Please, cold water, please . . ."

After a full minute of scrubbing and muttering, only a large dark-blue wet spot remained. But Salem wasn't finished. She now began removing all items from the table to the floor, muttering all the while: "They're gonna spill chocolate on my good tablecloth, my mother said. No they won't, I said. They will, she said. They're kids. Kids spill. They won't, I said. If they do, you're dead, she said. They won't, I said. They did . . ."

When all items were off, she swept the blue cloth from the table and stomped away. Within seconds, a washing machine could be heard churning to life. Salem returned with a stack of newspapers. She spread them over the table, then began transferring the items back from the floor. "*Little* kids spill, I said. *All* kids spill, she said. Not *these* kids, I said. My friends? Spill? Never. Hah! Ho-ho. I'm dead. Exterminated. I look like I'm alive. Here I am putting dishes on the table, but actually I'm a corpse. I am a dead eleven-year-old. Here lies Salem Jane Brownmiller . . . she trusted . . . she trusted . . . she's dead. . . ."

The last thing she did was return the four white

name cards to their former places. Except for the newspapers, the table now looked exactly as it had before.

The three guests, who had backed into the living room, dared return. Pickles applauded; Eddie and Sunny joined in. Salem took a deep breath, smiled for the first time in five minutes, and bowed briefly.

"You always get goofy when you're upset?" said Pickles, now staying well away from the copper pot.

"Only when I'm about to be executed by my own mother," said Salem. "Also, it helps me get things out of my system so I can return to normal."

"*Return* to normal?" Sunny chuckled. "How can you return if you were never *there*?"

Sunny laughed. Salem laughed. They all laughed.

"Find your places," said Salem. "It's time to eat."

17

Salem explained: "As I said, it's called fondue. You dip stuff in — *not* fingers. Look." At each place was a long, thin, two-pronged fork. Salem picked up hers, stabbed a strawberry, dipped it into the copper-potted chocolate, and held it up for all to see. "*Violà!*" She ate it. "Mmm-mm."

For the next five minutes the only sounds were the chewing of four mouths and the drip of chocolate onto newspaper. As the initial feeding frenzy slowed down, Pickles took time between bites to observe, "I am fond of fondue."

Eddie said as he downed the last of the pound-cake squares, "How did you know what to put out for dunking?"

"Chef's choice," said Salem. "I just decided what would go good with chocolate. And you're not dunking, you're dipping."

Eddie devoured his dripping dark-brown pound-cake square. "You mean you're allowed to dunk anything? It doesn't have to be what's here?"

Salem saw what was coming. She considered her answer carefully. "*Allowed?* Yes, you're allowed. There's no fondue law that says what you can and cannot dip. I mean, you're *allowed* to dip an eraser in the fondue. But that doesn't mean you *would*. That doesn't mean it would taste good." She decided to call his bluff, challenge him directly. "You wouldn't dip a brussels sprout in it, would you?"

Eddie made a face as he dipped a pretzel. "No *way*. Ugh."

"Well," said Salem, feeling a small puff of triumph, "it's all a matter of good taste."

Eddie licked chocolate from the pretzel before taking a bite. "How about pepperoni?"

In that instant, Salem knew she had brought a monster to life. She tried to ignore him. She gave no answer.

"Well?" said Sunny, grinning like a gremlin. "The boy asked about pepperoni."

Salem glared daggers at Sunny. "If the boy means is it *allowed* to dip pepperoni in chocolate fondue, yes, it is *allowed*, even though no sane or insane member of the human species would ever actually *want* to do it."

"I would," said Eddie cheerily.

Salem slumped. "No."

"You said there's no law."

"I also said it's a matter of good taste."

Eddie dipped a granola piece, then held it above

his open mouth to capture drippings. "Chocolate has good taste."

"Can't argue with that," Sunny added.

"Eddie," said Salem, "do you happen to remember a certain Saturday last month when you were here at this same table?"

Salem was referring to a lunch meeting she had called to discuss the question of a mascot for the new school. Eddie, the only one of the Principal's Posse to show up, had eaten virtually everything on the table and had wound up sick that night and all the next day.

"It wasn't the food I got sick on," said Eddie.

Salem jabbed her finger at him. "Don't you go saying it was my Periwinkle Punch."

Eddie shrugged and dipped a potato chip. "Okay, I won't say it."

Salem steamed. Eddie munched. Sunny watched. Pickles whispered to himself, "Periwinkle Punch."

Finally Salem began to slowly nod her head. "Okay . . . okay . . ." She got up from her chair, muttering, "Why should I care? It's not my life. Anyway, I'm already dead." She left the room. In a minute she returned with a saucer of pepperoni slices and a bucket. She placed the saucer in front of Eddie and the bucket on the floor beside him. She took her seat.

Eddie looked at the bucket. "What's that for?"

"For you to throw up in," Salem replied matter-of-factly, "if you'll excuse me ending the sentence with a preposition. When you fill that one up, I'll bring another."

Everyone but Salem laughed; Eddie ate. When he finished the chocolate-dipped pepperonis, he requested, and received, permission to check out the kitchen for further possibilities. He returned with string cheese, marshmallows, chocolate-frosted mini-donuts (They're *already* covered with chocolate! Salem thought but did not say), roast turkey, and a Swedish meatball.

"Yeuch!" went Sunny. She reached for the bucket. "He doesn't need this. I do."

Within a minute, Sunny, Salem, and Pickles had all retired to the living room. When Eddie finally joined them, the only sign of stomach distress he showed was a burp.

"Pig," said Salem.

Eddie took a seat in the recliner, pushed it back, put his feet up, burped again, and smiled contentedly. "So, what games are we going to play?"

"Games?" echoed Salem. "Do we have to play games? What is this, a first-grade birthday party?"

"Well, what did you have in mind?" said Sunny. "Sit around and discuss our favorite textbooks?"

Howls from Pickles and Eddie.

"So what do you want to play?" said Salem directly to Eddie. "Pin the tail on the donkey?"

"How about pin the tail on the hostess?" said Eddie.

More howls.

"How about pin the *kiss* on the hostess?" said Sunny.

Silence.

Quiet enough to hear Salem sizzling. Pickles noted her red face. "Sunnyburned?" he said.

Salem turned quickly to him, searching his face for meanness, but found only his usual friendly grin. She had to do something, change the picture. She popped up. "Egad, almost forgot! Sunny already saw my room but you guys didn't. First one who guesses what city it's supposed to be gets a copy of my first published book." She headed up the stairs. "Come on . . . come on . . . ."

By the time she led them back down the stairs (Pickles had quessed Paris), Salem had regained her composure. ". . . so we all expected the new coach to be another old macho gruff guy like Mr. Lujak, right, Eddie?"

"Right."

"So who shows up? Mr. Foy."

"The art teacher?" said Sunny.

"Exactly. And you knew he wasn't Mr. Lujak when he started out, 'Good afternoon, children.' "

Salem plopped onto the sofa. She shivered visibly. "Ouuu — don't you just hate to be called children?"

Eddie stretched out on the recliner. "Never thought about it."

"Well, we are, aren't we?" said Sunny.

"Who isn't?" said Pickles. "A hundred-year-old man is somebody's child."

"I know, I know," said Salem. "I'm not saying we aren't, technically. But you know what I mean. Like, they say a person becomes what you tell them they are. So if you call kids children and keep treating them like children, well, they'll act like children."

"That's so bad?" said Sunny. "I wouldn't want to act like some of the grown-ups I've seen."

"The point is," said Salem, "we're not in grade school anymore, where we were surrounded by little children. We're in middle school now, which means we'd better start growing up. Who knows what grown-up things are going to happen to us by the time we graduate from Plumstead three years from now. I say we start getting ready for grown-upness so it doesn't take us by surprise."

"So what should we do," said Pickles, "grow mustaches?"

Sunny said, "I know what she wants us to do." All heads swung to the dark-haired girl sitting cross-legged before the fireplace. "She wants us to start kissing."

18

This time Salem was ready.

"Listen to her, she keeps bringing up this kissing business. I was just thinking of the Halloween dance. That shows what's on *her* mind." She turned to Sunny. "Is there somebody in this room you wish to kiss, Miss Wyler?"

"Not me," said Sunny. "I'm too young for that stuff."

"Well, what are you going to do if some boy likes you? If he does kiss you?"

"He'd have to get close to me first, and that ain't gonna happen." Sunny tilted herself till she was lying on her side, her right arm propping up her head. "Unless he has five-foot-long lips."

Pickles roared at that one. Eddie laughed, but more carefully.

Salem jumped up, looked down at Sunny. "But what if he sneaks up on you, real quiet, from behind — " She demonstrated, playing the part of the boy with an invisible Sunny. "And then suddenly he goes — " She darted forward and planted a kiss on invisible Sunny's cheek.

Said the visible Sunny, "He'd be dead."

Eddie squirmed. Salem threw up her hands. "Well, see, that's what we're up against here. How can you have progress with that kind of attitude? You probably giggle every time somebody says the word *sex*."

"Don't you?"

Giggles from Eddie and Pickles.

"No," said Salem, "as a matter of fact, I don't. What's there to giggle about? It's nature. It's natural as trees and cows. Do you giggle when somebody says trees or cows?"

"If the tree tries to kiss the cow," said Sunny, "sure, absolutely."

Howls.

Salem gave a shrug of surrender. "Okay, okay, funny people, you win. I can see there's no point in trying to say something a little serious around here, not with a roomful of giggling little children." She returned to the sofa. "I guess I'll just go to the Halloween dance by myself. You'll probably be busy playing with your Tinker Toys anyway."

Salem folded her arms and stared grumpily at the floor.

Sunny sat up. She bobbed her head and batted her eyelashes. "I have an idea," she said perkily.

"Let's be big. Let's play spin the bottle!"

"Sunny," said Salem. "you can quit the act. Nobody believes it. And anyway, playing spin the bottle isn't being big."

Sunny stuck out her tongue at Salem.

Salem said, "My, my, such maturity. You know, Sunshine, you are a disgrace to your own sex when you act that way."

Sunny kept her tongue out while replying: "Ith that tho?"

"Yes, that's so. Everybody knows that girls mature faster than boys. It's okay for them" — she waved in Eddie's and Pickles' direction — "to act like babies, at least up to a point. They don't know any better." Eddie and Pickles looked at each other. "Something must be holding you back. Are you still eating Pablum by any chance?"

"No way," said Sunny, reeling in her tongue. "I eat mashed bananas. Doesn't everybody?"

"Hold it there," Pickles piped. "Back up a minute. That sounds like an insult to me. Who says I'm a baby?"

"You know what I mean," said Salem. "I didn't mean it as an insult. It's just nature's way. Girls mature faster than boys. In fact, women are usually more mature than men. That's why young women marry old men."

"Okay," said Pickles, "let's see who the baby is. Do you sleep with a night-light on?"

Salem scoffed, "Of course not." Suddenly she and Pickles locked eyes: Both had the same idea. "Hey," she said, "let's — "

" — ask everybody."

Salem stood. "Okay. Raise hands. Be honest, everybody. And anybody can ask a question. All right, same question: Who still sleeps with a nightlight on?"

All four looked around. One hand was in the air: Eddie's.

"Okay," said Pickles, "who's afraid to go down to the basement all by themselves?"

All eyes swung toward Eddie. Eddie's hands were gripping his chair. Then surprisingly, it was Pickles' hand in the air. "There's no use playing if we're not going to be honest."

The other three hands went up.

"All right," said Salem, "confession is good for the soul. Now we're getting somewhere." She thought. "Okay, how about this: Who still puts catsup on their scrambled eggs?"

Eddie raised his hand, puzzled. "What's wrong with that?"

Sunny said, "Ask him if he uses chocolate syrup."

Salem didn't ask, but the uncomfortable look on Eddie's face hinted at what the answer to that question might be.

"Next question," said Pickles. "Who still believes in the tooth fairy?"

No hands. Nevertheless, Salem, Sunny, and Pickles looked at Eddie and began to laugh. Again his face, especially his twitching nostrils, had given him away.

"*Who*," said Sunny, fixing her eyes on Salem, "is supposed to be a big-deal lady but can't even wiggle yet?"

Salem fumed at Sunny, then replied with a sniff, "The question has to apply to everyone in the room." She leaned toward Sunny. "*Who* . . . sticks out their tongue at people?"

Sunny smiled cheerfully, waved her hand in the air, and stuck out her tongue.

The questions came fast.

"Who eats peas with a spoon?"

Eddie raised his hand.

"Who gets sauce on themselves when they eat spaghetti?"

Eddie, Sunny, and Pickles.

"Who gets carsick?"

Nobody.

"Who cries when they get hurt?"

Everybody.

"Who sleeps with a stuffed animal?"

Eddie.

"Who," said Eddie, posing his first question, "has ever kissed a member of the opposite sex?"

Eddie shot his arm into the air, this time with pride. But so did the others.

"My father," snickered Salem, "you goof."

Eddie's hand came halfway down, he frowned; then his face brightened, his arm shot back up. "A member of the opposite sex who is not a relative!"

Sunny's and Pickles' hands went down. Salem's stayed up. "My mailman. When he brought me the letter that said I had a poem accepted in *Lickity Split*."

Eddie's arm strained for the ceiling. "A member of the opposite sex, not a relative, *your own age!*"

Everyone gaped at Eddie, whose chair had suddenly become a throne of triumph. Salem's hand went down. "Who?" she growled.

"Flossie," beamed Eddie.

The other three combed their brains.

"How old?" said Salem.

"Eleven, same as me."

"Lives in Cedar Grove?" said Pickles.

"Yep, definitely. Oh, yeah, I almost forgot — " Eddie put on a face of casual smugness — " *on the lips.*"

Stunned, staring silence was his tribute.

At last Salem rasped, "Flossie who?"

Eddie blinked, shrugged. "Flossie Mott."

Salem shrieked. "You said not a relative!"

"She's not a relative," said Eddie, and then it burst from him in howling laughter: "She's a *dog*! She's the same age as me and she kisses me all the time" — he pointed to his lips — "right *there!*"

Pickles cracked up. The two girls threw pillows at Eddie.

When things quieted down, Salem said, "All right, let's separate the adolescents from the babies. *Who* . . . will allow themselves to be kissed by another person in this room" — she glared at Sunny — "of the *opposite* sex, and in doing so will show he or she is the most mature person here?"

As Salem raised her hand, she looked about. No one else moved. "Well, I guess that settles that."

Sunny sat up straight. "No, I guess that *doesn't* settle that. Saying you'll do it doesn't prove anything. If somebody came over to give a big liplock, how do we know you wouldn't turn chicken and run off screaming in the other direction?"

Salem stared at Sunny. Salem stood. "Very well." She swallowed. "Okay." She swallowed again. She pinned her eyes on the picture hanging on the opposite wall; it was an oil painting of a clown with a sad face. She cleared her throat. "If someone would care to kiss me at this particular time, you may."

Somewhere outside little children squealed at play. In the Brownmiller living room, among the four still figures — three seated, one standing — all was as silent as the sad clown on the wall. As the silence grew longer, Salem fixed her eyes ever more on the picture. She sensed the distance between herself and the others increasing at an alarming rate, till they seemed no closer than orbiting moons. She had never felt so alone in her life. As her eyes began to water, the plump, drooping mouth of the clown blurred and overflowed and, perversely, seemed to turn up slightly as if beginning to smile.

And then someone was taking her hand — she turned — Pickles! — taking it and lifting it to his lips and kissing it — a light touch of his lips on the back of her hand, in the middle between her knuckles and wrist, letting her hand go then and returning to his seat.

For the next several moments Salem floated in a hazy daze. When she came to her senses, she found herself back on the sofa, and Sunny was standing before the fireplace, sneering, "Hah! That's nothing. You want to see *mature*? I'll show you *mature*. What's the big deal *allowing* yourself to be smooched? That's just being the smooch-*ee*. I want to know who's big enough to be the smooch-*er*. Who's got the nerve to walk over and lay a big wet one right on somebody's opposite-sex face right here in this room? Let's go — hands."

Salem did not move. Pickles did not move. Eddie did not move.

Sunny grinned. "Well, well." She raised her hand slowly, like a flag. "Looks like I'm surrounded by little kiddies."

What happened next happened very quickly. There was no time to react, only to stare wonderstruck. With a yip and a yelp, Sunny snatched up the hamster mask, rushed across the room to the boggle-eyed Eddie Mott, plunked the mask over his head and laid a loud, long, juicy smacker right on his three-inch whiskers. She then wheeled and hip-whipped back across the room, one hand fluffing up the back of her hair, fluttering her eyelids, crooning, "Just call me . . . Miss Ma-tur-i-tee . . ."

That's when everyone cracked up.

19

Halloween night!

Pickles was behind schedule. He had told the others he would pick them up at seven, and here it was already 7:05. He hadn't expected problems transferring his old bicycle headlight to the picklebus. Well, at least now it was done and working, ready for the dark.

What really got shortchanged was his costume. It had no distinctive finishing touches. He pulled the long green shroud over his head and let it fall to the floor. He pulled his arms in through the side slits. He looked in the mirror. He was not happy. Only a very sloppy eye would pass him for a pickle. He could just as easily go as a cactus, a cucumber, a green banana, or a moldy hot dog. Oh, well, there just wasn't time in a day to do everything right.

As Pickles pushed off toward Eddie's house, trick-or-treaters were dashing up the sidewalks and driveways, some with parents, some with bags as big as themselves. All along the street, doors were opening to reveal the silhouettes of tiny ghosts and goblins.

Pickles was torn.

On the one hand, he sort of agreed with Salem that they should all go to the dance. He agreed that they ought to support their school and that they were not little kiddies anymore and that the Halloween dance was as good a place as any to start growing up. Yes, he agreed with all that. Sort of.

But on the other hand, he would be lying if he said he didn't wish he were one of those kids dashing up and down the street. He asked himself what he would rather be holding that night: a girl on the dance floor or a bag full of candy? It was no contest.

That's what he was most uneasy about: the dance. And Salem. He had been uneasy for the three weeks since Salem's party, since he had kissed her hand. He kept wondering if she realized he had done it only to keep her feelings from being hurt. He wondered if she realized he wasn't ready yet to start messing around with girls.

Eddie stood before the bed in his Fruit of the Loom underwear. On the bed lay two Halloween costumes: Superman and a hobo. It was seven o'clock, Pickles would be here any second, and still he hadn't decided which one to wear.

It was amazing that Superman was even in the running, considering the flak he had caught over his red-and-blue underwear. But the fact was, Eddie had recently begun to calm down about the whole thing. Maybe it was cutting his hair that did it, getting it out of his system. Or maybe it was Sunny kissing him — well, the mask — even if she was joking. Or what Pickles had said to him one day: "Hey, man, stop trying to be somebody you're not. Be yourself."

Eddie had applied his best pal's advice to football. He stopped taking the game so seriously — not hard to do with Mr. Foy as a coach. Eddie didn't even object when Salem put happy face decals on everyone's helmet. And he joined the rest of the team in gorging himself silly during Salem's gourmet buffet time-outs. One game — incredibly! — she even brought chocolate fondue onto the field. Who cared that the Fighting Hamsters had lost their first four games by a combined score of 213 to 6?

As for goodies on this night, Mr. Brimlow had announced that there would be treats for the kids who came to the dance. Maybe so, but Eddie was willing to bet that they wouldn't give him enough stuff to cover his bed with, as he had done last year, and the year before that. He remembered wistfully how he had filled up his bag three times and had to keep coming back to the house to unload. He recalled fondly how sick he had gotten.

Every year, as far back as he could remember, he had gotten sick the day after Halloween. And why not? It was a tradition. What good was Halloween without enough junk to get sick on?

Ooguh! Ooguh!

Eddie heard the new picklehorn. He looked out. He couldn't see Pickles too well in the dark. The headlight switched on and off several times. "Pickle pickup!" came the call.

Eddie whirled to the bed. Be yourself, Pickles had said. Okay — who was he tonight? Superman or a hobo?

Superman!

He was dressed in thirty seconds and out the door.

Sunny was waiting on her front steps. The neighborhood was crawling with demons and monsters. What to be tonight had been no problem for her. She loved her hamster suit, even if the body part of it was a pair of Pickles' father's long underwear dyed caramel-brown and otherwise disguised. Her sole regret was that she had been allowed to wear it for only one game.

Ah, but what a game. It was against Harry S Truman Middle School. As the official Fighting Hamster, unseen behind her costume, she could get away with stuff that as a cheerleader she could not. In fact, shenanigans were expected of a mascot. So she roamed and cavorted at will, along the sideline and even into the bleachers. She led the cheers, she commanded the cheers, and if somebody wasn't cheering, she smacked them with her paw — and they laughed and cheered!

If only she could have confined herself to the spectators. If only she didn't want her school to win so bad. If only that Truman player wasn't laughing. There he was, running down the field, not a Hamster within twenty yards of him, heading for a sure touchdown with his team already ahead 47 to 0 — and he was *grinning*. That's what did it. Leading 47 to 0 and looking over at the Plumstead bleachers and grinning, rubbing it in. Well, he wasn't grinning when the four-foot-nine-inch hamster tackled him on the two-yard line.

Of course, they had to allow Truman a touchdown anyway. And of course Sunny had to be fired from her job. She wasn't too surprised at all that. What did surprise her, and disappoint her, was that the whole bleachers hadn't emptied and joined her in burying that Harry S Truman grinner.

Ooguh! Ooguh! "Pickle pickup! Pickle pickup!"

Still a block away, the picklebus clattered down the sidewalk, its headlight like a low-flying star. Sunny ran out to meet it.

Two years before Salem had been William Shakespeare. Last year she was Louisa May Alcott (even if nobody realized it). And this year: a beatnik poet, all black from her floppy felt hat to her cape to her boots. She seldom fooled anyone on Halloween. Everyone knew that the Brown-miller girl would be the one in the writer's getup.

Lately, Salem was wondering if she had been fooling herself. When Pickles kissed her hand at the party, she had been stunned. No surprise there. But there had also been a second reaction, and it *was* a surprise: fright. It had scared her to be that close to a boy, to wonder what was next, to have used her female powers to cause a boy to act.

Until then, she had only imagined what it would be like to be more than just friends with Pickles. Now she had discovered that imagination could not always be trusted. It frightened her to think that she could be responsible for someone else's feelings, for making them happy or sad. It scared her to think that things might get complicated at the dance tonight. What if Pickles tried to kiss her again, this time not on the hand? What could she say to him without hurting him? How could she make him understand that she liked the two of them just the way they were? How could she tell him that she wasn't ready yet to start getting personal with boys?

Ooguh! Ooguh!

Salem opened her front door. All three of them yelled: "Pickle pickup! Pickle pickup!"

For a moment she just stood there. What a

sight: two pickles — one horizontal, one upright — a superhero and a hamster. She couldn't help giggling. What was there to be afraid of?

"What are you supposed to be?" called Sunny. "A lump of coal?"

"I'm a beatnik!" called Salem. She shut the door behind her and climbed aboard.

The Pickle Posse was still five blocks from school when Eddie cried out: "Ou-ou, stop!"

The bus came to a halt.

"*That* house." Eddie pointed to a house across the street. The door was open. One group of Halloweeners was leaving, one group could be seen in the living room, one was waiting on the porch, and another was heading up the driveway. "They give the best stuff," Eddie gushed. "They give candy, and not the mini-sizes. The *regular* sizes. And if you ask for two, you *got* it!"

"You come this far for Halloween?" said Pickles.

"I go everywhere," said Eddie, who already had both feet on the sidewalk. "I know that house. I gotta go." He looked at his friends. "I *gotta.*"

"Well," said Sunny, "if you gotta, you gotta." From somewhere inside her hamster suit she pulled a pillowcase. She handed it to Eddie. "And if *you* gotta" — she pulled out three more and waved them in the air — then we *all* gotta!"

Everyone cheered and grabbed a pillowcase.

The picklebus zoomed across the street.

As they headed for the open door, Eddie raved on: "And I know another great house on Beech Street . . . and one on Woodbine . . ."

The picklebus never made it to the school dance.

About the Author

Jerry Spinelli was born in Norristown, Pennsylvania. He attended Gettysburg College and The Writing Seminars at Johns Hopkins University. His novels include *Maniac Magee*, which won the Newberry Medal, *Fourth Grade Rats*, and *Report to the Principal's Office*, the first in the School Daze series. He lives in Phoenixville, Pennsylvania, with his wife and fellow author, Eileen Spinelli, and sons, Sean and Ben.

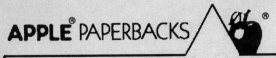

APPLE® PAPERBACKS

Pick an Apple and Polish Off Some Great Reading!

BEST-SELLING APPLE TITLES

❏ MT43944-8 **Afternoon of the Elves** Janet Taylor Lisle $2.75

❏ MT43109-9 **Boys Are Yucko** Anna Grossnickle Hines $2.75

❏ MT43473-X **The Broccoli Tapes** Jan Slepian $2.95

❏ MT42709-1 **Christina's Ghost** Betty Ren Wright $2.75

❏ MT43461-6 **The Dollhouse Murders** Betty Ren Wright $2.75

❏ MT43444-6 **Ghosts Beneath Our Feet** Betty Ren Wright $2.75

❏ MT44351-8 **Help! I'm a Prisoner in the Library** Eth Clifford $2.75

❏ MT44567-7 **Leah's Song** Eth Clifford $2.75

❏ MT43618-X **Me and Katie (The Pest)** Ann M. Martin $2.75

❏ MT41529-8 **My Sister, The Creep** Candice F. Ransom $2.75

❏ MT42883-7 **Sixth Grade Can Really Kill You** Barthe DeClements $2.75

❏ MT40409-1 **Sixth Grade Secrets** Louis Sachar $2.75

❏ MT42882-9 **Sixth Grade Sleepover** Eve Bunting $2.75

❏ MT41732-0 **Too Many Murphys** Colleen O'Shaughnessy McKenna $2.75

Available wherever you buy books, or use this order form.

Scholastic Inc., P.O. Box 7502, 2931 East McCarty Street, Jefferson City, MO 65102

Please send me the books I have checked above. I am enclosing $_____ (please add $2.00 to cover shipping and handling). Send check or money order — no cash or C.O.D.s please.

Name _____

Address _____

City _____ **State/Zip** _____

Please allow four to six weeks for delivery. Offer good in the U.S.A. only. Sorry, mail orders are not available to residents of Canada. Prices subject to change.

APP591

THE BABY-SITTERS CLUB®

Collect Them All!

by Ann M. Martin

The seven girls at Stoneybrook Middle School get into all kinds of adventures...with school, boys, and, of course, baby-sitting!

APPLE® PAPERBACKS

THE GYMNASTS™

by Elizabeth Levy